The Art Of Crime

A Stephi Cay Paranormal Mystery

A Novel by
Kimberly Seba

This book is dedicated to the loving memory of my mom Linda "Nana" Hibbard, my childhood friend Doug "Dougie" Estes, and my former husband William "Bill" James Diehl II, three of the most respected and beloved police officers who worked as policemen and who I will admire forever.

And to my children, Cassandra, Stephanie, Ronnie Jr, and Bryan – you are special to me, and I love you all.

And to all my grandchildren, I hope this book shows that if you put your mind to it, you can do anything. Love you all, Nani.

Prologue

Do you ever think what life-altering events will change you forever? How that one event will determine how you perceive the world? I'm not talking about the little everyday stuff that happens throughout one's life. The life-changing events are intertwined with the supernatural. There was a time when I didn't think anything could infiltrate my world.

I was married to my soul mate, we had a beautiful daughter, a nice home, and a moderate income. We weren't poor, but we weren't filthy rich either. We were, as Goldilocks says, 'just right!' That was our life. Just right!

It was perfect, well as perfect as perfect could be, because in reality, nothing in life is completely perfect. Right? This was proven when the sudden death of my husband ripped a hole in our perfect little world. I thought I would never make it through that dark time in my life. And I wouldn't have, if not for my daughter. She was my light, my hope and the reason I became a Private Investigator. I wanted to give up on life, on my career, everything. I can't tell you how many times my daughter would say 'No, dad will be sad if you just give up and so will I'. And she was right. He would be sad. So, I pushed through it, but the nightmares persisted even today they haunt me.

I thought losing my husband would be the only life-altering event I would see in my lifetime. I was wrong. I was about to experience a second one and this one was a doozy!

Chapter One

I pulled the curtains open to let in the beautiful spring day, drinking in the warm sun. It was going to be a beautiful day. It was spring, flowers were blooming, the leaves on the trees were changing from yellow to green, and all was right in the world. As I slowly opened my eyes the familiar blue 1980 Ford pickup my husband Bill was driving, which he refused to get rid of, was pulling into the driveway. Finally! He was home. We had a huge day planned. Now we could start decorating for our daughter's surprise birthday party. The plan was perfect. While my mom picked her up from school, and stalled her by taking her to get a shake, we would put up the decorations. She didn't have many school friends, but the few she did have were the best. We invited them along with a few of our friends so it would look like a big party. Bill had gone to buy all the stuff we needed so I ran to the front door to go help bring everything in. With my luck, he would drop the cake just so he wouldn't drop the decorations. I yanked it open and went to push on the screen door, it didn't budge. I pushed again. Nothing. I started to yank vigorously back and forth. I looked out at Bill and watched as his tall, lean frame strolled toward me with that sexy saunter that would bring any woman to her knees. And when he was in his uniform, it would make you faint. He smiled when he saw me, and I felt my heart race so fast I thought it would explode from my chest. I smiled back, vigorously waving at him. I tried to yell at him that the door was stuck, but nothing came out. He could look at it later, he was quite the handyman. I was so happy to see him, I missed him so much. It seemed like forever since he'd been gone. Just on the off chance it was the user, which normally was with me, and not the door, I yanked on the door one more time with so much force it was like I had super strength. It knocked me back, I shook my head ready to tackle the door again when suddenly the screen door started to slowly creep open, squealing as it did so. Finally! I thought. I moved toward the open door to meet him halfway but when I got to the threshold I started to fall forward. I quickly grabbed the door frame to balance myself. I looked down at my feet willing them to move. I tried lifting, then jerking each leg frantically, but they wouldn't budge. It was like someone had put super glue on the bottom of my shoes. Why couldn't I move? I needed to get to him. I looked up, his outstretched arms were beckoning me to be wrapped in his warmth and safety. "Bill. I can't move!" I yelled, shocked that words actually came out, while still struggling to release my feet from their prison. I held out my hand and screamed, 'Bill!' He smiled, blew me a kiss and waved, then turned and slid into his car. "No, Bill! No! Come back!" In an instant, he was gone. Again. I slid down the door frame into a fetal position and began to cry.

***

Nothing gets the heart pumping like a loud bang early in the morning. Lucky me, I heard three! The dream, or more like a dreammare, slowly faded away and reality took its place. Three more bangs and poof the dream was a distant memory. My brain, still somewhere between the dream world and reality, mistook the bangs as gunshots. I bolted straight up in bed, my breathing heavy, and immediately reached for the Colt 45 that slept under my pillow. Ignoring the sweat dripping down my face, I eased my finger over the safety lock, ready to flip and fire. I scanned the room. Everything was in place; the bedroom door was closed, and the windows locked tight. I felt the cold grip of paranoia start to subside. My arms slumped between my legs. Wiping the sweat from my face, I heard the reason I was stripped from my dream.

"Mom! You up?" Riley shouted through the door.

Seriously! Why does she have to do that? "Wouldn't a gentle knock suffice? Or maybe an easy shake to wake me up," I mumbled to myself. Oh no, it was much more fun to scare the bejesus out of me. I carefully placed the Colt back under my pillow, "Yeah, I'm up", I replied groggily and slumped back on the pillow.

"Good, because Nana said you better get your butt downstairs, fast!"

I waved my arm as if trying to air-grab something with my eyes closed. Oh, wait, my eyes were closed. I could hear Riley thud across the wood floors of the hallway and shout, "Love you!" as she thudded down the stairs. A mental picture of this popped into my head as I smiled and whispered, "Love you too."

Eyes still closed, I threw back the sheets but refused to budge. Why did the weekends have to end so quickly? I thought about Riley. My seventeen-year-old who could be a nightmare at times, was the one constant that kept me from losing my mind after the death of her father. She was strong, smart, beautiful, loving, and caring. But when crossed, she was a spitfire. I chuckled. Yeah, she got that from her Nana. And, of course, she knew everything like every other teenager on the planet. We shared the same blue eyes, turned-up nose and full lips, but she had struck gold getting her dad's sandy blonde hair.

Ugh!! I just want to throw the sheets back over me and sleep until Riley got out of school. Riley. I smiled again. Riley! My eyes shot open, and I jerked my head toward the beaming red numbers on the digital clock sitting annoyingly on the nightstand. 6:30 am! What the hell! Did I forget to set the alarm? No wonder Riley was banging on my door.

I reluctantly pulled myself up and headed for the bathroom. I looked in the mirror. My long, ash-brown hair looked like I stuck my finger in a light socket. My best feature, eyes as blue as a Texas sky, seemed darker with the black circle's underneath. I could literally be an extra on The Walking Dead as a zombie! Thank you, Texas pollen and the Gulf of Mexico, for blowing all this crap into Springfield, and straight into my nasal passages!

I reached over and turned on the shower. I needed it hotter than normal this morning to clear out the gunk clogged inside these nasal passages. With Riley's warning from Nana still branded on my brain, I quickly showered, taking a few extra seconds to let the hot water flow over my face. I threw myself into the usual work attire. Dark blue t-shirt, black jacket, jeans and, of course, my favorite Doc M black boots. Thank goodness for my naturally wavy hair, there was no need for all that extra hair stuff, I pulled my hair into a ponytail. Not one to wear a lot of makeup, I slapped on some base and mascara. I slipped on my black leather belt, threaded my holster onto it and retrieved my Colt 45. I shoved my cell phone in one pocket and my ID in the other. One last glance at the digital clock beamed 6:47 am. I smiled…nailed it!

As I made my way down the stairs to the kitchen, I could hear the usual morning chatter between Nana and Riley. It was music to my ears, the casual banter between them. My mom, Raylan Lane, one of the best Detective Sergeants in the Springfield police department, was now retired and helped me run the Lane Private Investigation Agency we started three years ago. Lovingly referred to as Nana by everyone she knew, she is a piece of work. Always on everyone's case, nagging about how to raise Riley, what to wear, what to eat, that I need a man in my life…blah, blah, blah.

"Well, look who decided to join the living", Nana said with as much sarcasm as a bottomless pit.

"Morning mom," Riley said in between bites of her eggs and toast while playing a game on her cell phone.

Seriously? Why can't I multi-task like that?

"Morning baby girl," I said kissing the top of her head.

"Good morning to you as well grumpy," I said to Nana as I made a beeline to the Keurig on the counter. Ah, my Keurig...my java lifeline. Whoever invented this machine is my hero for life and definitely deserves some kind of award or something. I took my favorite mug from the cabinet and placed it accordingly on the machine. Riley had already made her usual Breakfast Blend, so I checked the water reservoir to see if it needed filling. She actually left me some in there, huh. Usually, she used all the water and wouldn't fill it up for the next person...me! Luckily, I didn't have to do much but drop in my French Vanilla.

As the machine worked its magic, I leaned against the counter and stared at my mom. A hard life and two bouts of cancer had taken its toll on her. Gray had replaced her dark brown locks and pain lines slithered across her face like snakes. I loved and admired this woman more than words could say. As I smiled at this thought I asked, "Have you checked the messages for any new cases?" All calls to the office were transferred to the landline at home when the office was closed.

She turned from the stove, "We got a call from a Mr. Pittman from State Insurance Company. One of their clients, the Avery Art Museum, had an expensive piece of Art stolen." She turned back to swishing the eggs in the skillet. "I didn't call them back because I had to wait for *someone* to get their pretty little butt downstairs. So, you have the honors," she said waving the spatula behind her head.

Well, so much for a relaxing cup of coffee and breakfast before work. Rarely did I eat breakfast, but this morning I *really* wanted some eggs. And they smelled yummy. Had she added a new spice? Paprika? Once I had thought about trying out for one of the cooking shows we watched regularly, but that was before Bill's death. Well, at least I could eat toast on the road. I grabbed one from the plate on the table, a to-go cup from the cabinet and poured my java lifeline into it.

"C'mon baby girl, let's blow this joint. You've got school in twenty minutes." As Riley gathered her school paraphernalia, I strode over to grumpy and gave her a kiss on the cheek. "Love you. I'll see you at the office, yes?"

"Pfft, of course. Who else is gonna run the place while you're out chasing bad guys"? She grinned and said, "Love you too."

Riley gave her grandmother a quick kiss on the cheek, "Love you Nana!" she said and bolted for the door. I shook my head as I followed her out. Every morning to avoid her Nana nagging her on the dos and don'ts of high school she turned into Speedy Gonzales. One morning after a late night of studying and still too groggy to even speak and that was after coffee. Well, my mom wasn't about to pass up an opportunity. Nana swooped in like a vulture on a dying carcass. She started lecturing on the importance of a good night sleep, how it affects the performance at school, blah…blah…blah. Riley just sat there half asleep and took it like a trooper. Luckily she didn't have to take it for long, she was literally saved by the doorbell.

Riley had just stepped into the school when it started to rain. Perfect! My umbrella was sitting happily dry at home while I

7

would be getting pounded by the weather. By the time I made it to the office, which sat in a small strip center on the west side of Springfield, the rain had stopped, and the sun was shining. Yep, typical Texas weather. It was a known fact that if you lived in Texas, especially near the coast, it could go through all four seasons in the span of ten minutes. I parked my baby, a 1965 apple red Mustang, in the rear of the office and headed inside the back entrance. After the usual routine of shutting off the alarm, flipping on lights, turning on the Keurig…yeah, I got one at the office too…. I switched the phones back to office mode. The office didn't open until nine, and mom wouldn't show up until few minutes before, so I had some time to make me another java lifeline and make some phone calls. Just as I got settled at my desk, the phone rang. I looked at the caller ID which read State Insurance Agency. Okeydokey, one less call to make.

"Lane Private Detective Agency, Stephie Cay speaking," I said in my professional voice.

"Finally! Ms. Cay, this is Argus Pittman from the State Insurance Company," he began. His voice sounded urgent…or was that desperate? "I glad you're there."

Finally, I thought, and glanced over at the answering machine. The number ten blinked rapidly at me. Ok, urgent *and* desperate!

"Yes, Mr. Pittman, I was about to call you. My apologies, I didn't have a chance to listen to your message. How can I help you?"

"We are calling to retain your Agency to investigate a theft at the Avery Art Museum before we pay out on the policy," he began. "We *really* need your expertise."

8

"Surely the Art Museum filed a report on the theft?" Which I knew was standard procedure. And added, "Didn't the police investigate?"

"Yes, of course," he said, "but my client wishes to keep this incident as quiet as possible, and he specifically asked for your agency. He feels the police will not work as quickly."

Mom kept in touch with her buddies from the station, so I knew they would've already sent someone, especially since the theft was from one of Springfield's founding families, the Avery's. Why would he need a P.I. for something the police could handle? I had a gut feeling there was a lot more to this case than he was letting on which makes sense for the lame excuse he was giving. Nevertheless, it should be pretty cut and dry, so I inform Mr. Pittman we'll take the case and that my retainer fee was ten percent of the recovered property, plus expenses. He said that was not a problem. "Can you fill me in on any other details?"

"Well," he hesitated, "all we can say is the painting is worth $300,000," then said as if it were an afterthought, "and was taken some time between 9:00 pm Thursday night and 7:00 am Friday morning."

Why did he keep referring to himself as we? Was he talking about the insurance company? That seemed odd. Why not just say 'I'? Letting it slide, I asked, "Who do I need to speak with at the museum?"

"Brian Williams is the Head Curator, however, he is currently out of the country. You will need to speak with his Assistant Curator, Angela Gates," he offered, then added. "We want to thank you, Ms. Cay for accepting the case. We know your agency will work quickly and efficiently."

9

"You're welcome, Mr. Pittman. We will do everything we can to recover the stolen painting. As soon as I know anything more, we will contact you." As we were saying our goodbyes Nana strolled in the back entrance. I filled her in on my conversation with Mr. Pittman and told her of my suspicions while doing a little research on the computer. Why was he hesitant to give me the information I needed to help solve the case? Like what type of painting, where it was from, how much it was worth. Shouldn't he have spilled his guts? Especially since he was so hell-bent on getting in touch with us.

Something else kept nagging me about another case like this one, but I couldn't put my finger on it. I would have to research it later. Right now, we needed to get over to the museum.

Chapter Two

The Avery Art Museum was located on the east side of Springfield's Old Towne district. Mr. Avery, an avid art collector, had restored his family's home and made it into an art museum. The Avery's were one of the founding families of Springfield so most of the collection consisted of pieces he had collected or inherited. Mixed in were pieces from new artists. Joseph Phillip Avery, a tall handsome and rich, man in his early fifties, with salt and pepper hair, and in very good shape, now resided in New York. Females who grew up in Springfield knew these few *delicious* details. I was one of them. He was a looker for sure, but when he spoke his true colors emerged. He was filthy rich, and he knew it.

Over the years, the sleepy town of Springfield had gotten a reputation for being a great place to live, raise a family and had grown quickly into a full-fledged city. It had survived three major hurricanes, two of which almost annihilated it. After the first storm, most of the residence relocated further inland, but the ones that remained, which included the Lane's and the Avery's, rebuilt. A second, even stronger storm fifteen years later devastated the town again. Once more, the town was rebuilt. And every time the Avery family had donated to its reconstruction.

When the city council decided to restore the original site of the old town, of which the Avery family home was a part of that restoration, Mr. Avery had donated the funding for the project. He might be a snob, but he loved this city and would do anything for it.

My mom loved old houses. She had carefully hand-picked her own house, which also sat in the old town site. Restoring it to its former glory had taken nearly all my life, but she had finished it. I smiled. I was very proud of her for that accomplishment. So here we sat, in front of the museum, looking at the architectural design instead of investigating. As if I were blind, she started describing it…'the main part of the house is wood, see just there…oh, and look how beautiful those two long, arch-shaped windows on either side of blue gabled roof that has one long, arched window in the center', just over there. "Do you see, Stephi?" I could feel her boring a hole in the side of my head and glanced out of the corner of my eye to find I had been busted looking at my phone.

"Finished?" I asked coolly. She gave me a disgusted look that said 'Whatever?'

We got out and headed up the small porch that was supported by two pillars that had black iron railing attached to the concrete steps that took us to ornate French doors.

As we entered, a concierge desk sat perfectly in the center of the main hall. A young woman who looked to be in her mid-twenties, dark brown hair pulled neatly in a bun, wearing *way* too much jewelry, smiled, and said, "Welcome to the Avery Art Museum. How may I help you?"

"We are here to speak with Angela Gates, please," I said.

"And you are?" She said, politely, but defensively.

"My name is Stephi Cay," I gestured toward Nana, "and this is Raylan Lane. We are with the Lane Private Detective Agency."

She looked at us a little shocked, scared almost and said, "Um, yes…one moment please." She punched a few buttons on the phone, and I glanced over at Nana. We were both thinking the same thing. Odd reaction.

While she called Ms. Gates, Nana and I glanced around the main hall of the museum. There were curved wooden staircases on both sides of the concierge desk. I assumed they led to the actual museum. On the right as you walk in, was a souvenir shop. On the left wall hung beautiful paintings that cascaded up the staircase as though they were leading you somewhere wonderful and magical.

"Ms. Gates will be with you shortly," the young woman informed us and immediately returned to her work.

Well, all right then. I thanked her even though I knew she was clearly done with us. "That was a strange reaction, right?" She nodded agreement, but before she could comment, we were greeted by Angela Gates who appeared surprised we were here. She was tall, looked to be about 5' 10", thin and had blonde hair that obviously wasn't the color she was born with. "Angela Gates, Assistant Curator, how can I help you?" she asked, shaking both our hands, and quickly added, "Are you working with the Police Department?"

"Uh, no", I said, glancing briefly at Nana, "we have been retained by State Insurance Company at the request of Mr. Avery to investigate the theft that occurred here last Thursday."

"My apologies", she said with a nervous smile, "I was not informed the insurance company would be sending in a private investigation team".

Really? Apparently, the "we" Mr. Pitman spoke of was not anyone associated with the Art Museum. "No need for apologies," I assured her, "we were just retained this morning." I looked at Nana, who was being way too quiet, giving Angela her suspicious face. I elbowed her and she looked at me as if to say 'what'. "Do you mind answering a few questions?"

"Of course not," she said, "please follow me."

We nodded and followed her through double doors on the left and down a long corridor behind the concierge desk. We entered one of the doors on the left. I scanned the room, noticing many certificates and awards. The décor resonated the era the house was initially built. Her desk donned a laptop, family pictures, all the normal items found on a desk and a stack of papers. In front of her desk sat two mahogany high-back leather chairs. Angela walked behind her desk and motioned for us to sit.

Sitting, she said nervously, "I have to admit Ms. Cay," then to Nana, "Ms. Lane. I'm a little perplexed as to why you are here." Her hands were clasp together on the desk and upon her next statement, she began to fidget. "I have already told the police everything I know, surely you can acquire the information from them?" Until now, she had made eye contact with us. And then she looked off to her left as if she were talking to an invisible person and whispered, "I *do not* understand why I should have to go through this again!"

Nana and I glanced at each other, both thinking the same thing. RED FLAG! Okay, suspect number one? I would be checking her out more thoroughly. Why would she be so nervous about repeating what she told the police? Was she afraid the information she gave us wouldn't coincide with the police report?

"Um, okay," I said, and bringing the conversation back into reality, "Is it possible to get a list of employees that work at the museum?"

She nodded, still looking as though she were in la-la land and began typing on her laptop. In seconds she had the information printed. "I can only give you names, no other information." As she handed me the printout she added, "Now, I'm afraid I must conclude our conversation. I have a conference call in fifteen minutes."

Cutting us off, acting strangely…if she was involved, she wasn't doing a good job of hiding it. And for someone who was perplexed as to why we were there, she didn't hesitate to give us the employee list. "May we see the crime scene?" Did she just roll her eyes at me like a five-year-old? Reluctantly she stood and motioned for us to follow her.

We followed Angela back into the main hall and took the stairs on the right with the cascading paintings. Upon reaching the top, the staircases merged and opened into a large room with more paintings lined around the walls. We walked toward the back of the room where the crime had taken place. There was an empty space where the stolen painting once hung, now surrounded by crime scene tape. I scanned the room for signs of security cameras but saw nothing with the naked eye. Okay, there are obviously hidden cameras, but I asked anyway, "Do you have security cameras?"

"Of course," Angela said facing me. "We have four, one in each corner of the room and one overhead," she pointed toward the ceiling," that captures any hidden areas."

"Could we see the security tape from the day of the robbery?" Nana asked.

"There is only one copy, and the police have it as evidence," she replied, apparently annoyed that we would ask a question we should already know. She was seriously getting on my last nerve with her attitude. I got plenty of that from Riley, I didn't need it from this woman.

Nana and I looked at each other and nodded. We both knew she would have no problem getting a copy from Dougie at the station. Once we had a copy, our whiz kid, Riley could look at it. Riley had a knack for seeing details that any normal person would miss, like she had a sixth sense or something. Nana claims she acquired this talent from her…which she probably did. Actually, we both did.

"Can you tell us what type of painting was stolen?" Nana asked. "Rembrandt, Gogh?"

Angela looked at her and scoffed. "The painting stolen is worth far more than any of *those* paintings." Oh, really, I thought. Something worth more than a Rembrandt or Gogh?

"Okay," Nana said, getting irritated at this point. "So *what* painting is worth more than one of those?"

"Why, the portrait of Mr. Avery's sister, of course?" She shook her head as if we were supposed to know this.

"Wait, what?" I asked. "Mr. Avery has a sister?" I had literally read everything on Joseph Avery growing up and nothing mentioned he had a sister. "There must be some mistake."

Angela shook her head, "No mistake, Ms. Cay."

Nana nudged me before bringing the conversation back to reality, then asked, "Is anyone ever left alone in the building?" Angela adamantly replied that *no one* is ever left alone. There was always a security guard left with the janitor and they usually leave around ten o'clock.

"Who was here after closing last Thursday?" I ask glancing at the list of employees. Angela informed us that she was here until about eight forty-five, catching up on paperwork. After that, it was

16

one of their security guards, Walter Mayhew, and the janitor, Paul Bailey. Everyone else had left between seven forty-five and eight.

"Did you notice anything suspicious before you left?" Nana inquired.

"No, but I was in my office most of the time. I do, however, always make one final walk-through before leaving and all the paintings were in place. Now, if you will excuse me, I have a conference call." I thanked her for her time and added we would likely be back later. I want Riley to use her keen senses to check out the crime scene.

By the time we left the museum, it was close to noon. Riley had a short school day due to finals, so that would be our first stop. Before the car doors shut, Nana had her cell phone out punching the number to her ex-partner Springfield PD Detective Eugene Douglas. Dougie, as we like to call him, had always been more than a partner to Nana, he was family. Dougie and I were friends mainly through his sister, who was one of my best friends growing up.

After retrieving Riley from school, we were all in agreement that sustenance was our top priority. Me especially since my breakfast consisted only of a piece of toast. We headed for our favorite place, Burger Joint. No, really! That's what Sam named it. When I say joint, that's exactly what I mean. It's been in the same place with the same furniture and the same owners since I was a little girl. But it still puts out the best food in town. Sam, the owner, was a sweet, kind old man who had a thing for Nana. If she wanted poop burgers, he'd find a way to make one. It was cute in a way, but way over the top.

Upon seeing us, Sam shot over to open the door for us, well actually for Nana.

"Good afternoon to three of the most beautiful girls in all of Springfield!" Sam said cheerfully. We greet him in unison. He put his hand on Nana elbow gently guiding her to the counter before rushing behind the rugged-looking counter again.

"What can I get you today?" he asked, looking at me and Riley. We order cheeseburgers, fries and cokes. Sam, the biggest, harmless, flirt in town, leans over the counter and with googly eyes (What? That's the only way to describe it!), asks Nana, "And what can I get you pretty lady?" Nana giggled and shooed him away. Yes, even at her age it's possible. Riley and I looked at each other and snickered. She has been saying, like forever, that she is tired of looking like a beached whale, so she orders a chicken caesar salad and ice water. Riley and I look at each other and put our fist out for rock, paper, scissors. We know full well one of *us* will be eating that salad. Nana suddenly turns around and we axe the rock, paper, scissors. As we headed to a table, I secretly hoped it was Riley and I'm pretty sure she hoped it was me.

We found an empty wooden table, which looked more like a picnic table, and sat down. Now we all knew sitting at these old wooden tables could be hazardous to your health and there was an art to it. See, you wanna sit down softly so as not to break the bench in half and you *never, ever* slide your butt across due to the great possibility of picking up a few splinters. Ah, but the food was well worth the danger. Sam delivered our food in record time. He placed Nana's down last giving her a smile and a wink. She smiled and waved at him. Seriously? I'm about to eat here!

I scoop up my burger, mouth open ready to savor the yumminess when I glance at Nana. First mistake. Her eyes were fixated on my fries. Second mistake, never offer one French fry to a woman eating nothing but a salad. "Would you like one of my fries?"

A huge smile eased across her face, or maybe that was a grin. Being the good daughter I am, I switched my burger from two hands to one hand and lifted the basket over the table so she could get one. She snatched the entire basket nearly pulling my arm out of the socket. Then her eyes fixed on my burger. Third mistake, after having your fries snatched from you, don't offer your burger to a woman eating nothing but a salad.

"What?" I say sarcastically, "Now you want my burger too?"

"Aw, thank you, Stephi, for sharing your burger and fries. You're such a good daughter," she slides the salad in front of me. I look over at Riley who was halfway done with her burger. She looked at me with a mouthful of yumminess, smiled and shrugged. I gave her the "thanks a lot. pal" look.

"I suppose you want my coke, too?"

Nana took a bite of *my* burger and says, "Of course not, cokes are fattening."

I rolled my eyes. Well, at least I ended up with *my* coke. Geez, her diets were not working well for her, but they were working miracles for me! With all the food shuffling finished, we quickly brought Riley up to speed on what we had learned so far. Picking at my salad I ask Nana what Dougie had said.

"Oh, we had a good chat," she began, taking a bite of 'my' burger, "he said he didn't care too much for his new rookie partner, which, naturally, made me feel good," she picked up a fry and popped it in her mouth. "He told the Chief he wanted a raise if he had to endure working with this goober." Nana laughed to herself at this, then continued, "He did fuss at me for retiring and blamed me for getting stuck with the rookie. Oh, and we have a lunch date next week."

Riley and I stare at her. Seriously? "Ma! What did he say about *the case*?" She knew when I called her Ma, instead of Nana, that I was annoyed.

"Oh, my bad," she said chuckling. "Doug said he would look at the case file and get a copy of the tape. He also said he would call us with any new developments."

Okay, that was a start. Our next stop would be the museum again to interview the employees and see if we can get more intel on this supposed daughter and her painting. As it stood right now, they were all suspects. I paid our check, and with my stomach still aching for a friggin' burger and fries, we hopped into Nana's car and headed back to the museum.

Chapter Three

It was a given, if Riley was riding with us then we brought Nana's car, a black Ford Crown Victoria, because my old jalopy...as my darling daughter so rudely called it...didn't have Sirius radio, which meant she had to listen to my Queen cd's, which meant unbridled torture for Nana because she couldn't listen to her oldies. Me, I have a rather eclectic music taste, so I wasn't put out too much. And well, let's be honest, rockin' out to Queen is way cooler in a Mustang than a Crown Victoria.

We arrived back at the museum a little after two and were met by a black limousine parked in front. "Mr. Avery is obviously here," I heard a sigh of disgust come from Nana sitting next to me. Those two had a history and it wasn't a pleasant one. I parked next to the limo, well actually in front of it seeing as it took up space across almost four parking spots. Shouldn't he have his own personal parking on the side? As we entered the museum, we were immediately met by the same woman that sat behind the concierge desk on our first visit. She introduced herself as Brynn Lewis and informed us Ms. Gates asked her to help us with whatever we needed.

"Has she left for the day?" Nana asked.

"She is, um, on a very important conference call," Brynn said nervously, "What can I help you with?"

Again? How many conference calls can one person have in a day? "We need to see the crime scene again please."

Brynn nodded at me. As we followed her up to the second floor, I asked, "After we look around, we'd like to interview the security guard on duty the evening of the theft."

"Yes, of course," she said nervously. "That would be Mike Irwin. He should be in later."

Riley and Nana headed straight for the crime scene. I started to follow, but instead glanced back at the young lady. "May I ask you a question?" When she nodded an agreement, I continued. "Can you tell me what painting was stolen?"

"I-I'm not allowed to discuss that ma'am." She instantly became nervous, looking over her shoulder. Now, I knew all too well what painting had been stolen having asked Angela Gates earlier. My question was meant to garner a reaction. And I got a doozy.

"Sorry, but I don't understand. Why can't you discuss it?"

Her eyes wide as ping pong balls, she ignored my question and continued to look over her shoulder while nervously rubbing her hands together. She had gone from anxious to terrified in a split second. She even had pellets of sweat on her forehead. Not wanting to stress the poor girl out to the point of psychiatric help, I let her off the hook.

"You don't have to stay Ms. Lewis," I said, placing my hand on her shoulder. "Here's my card. If you remember anything, please call". With a quick nod and half smile, she turned and high-tailed it out of the room. What on earth is making these people crazy nervous when any questions are asked about this painting?

As I joined the team, Riley had already made a beeline inside the crime scene tape and was checking the wall around where the painting once hung. Nana, on the other hand, was walking along the perimeter of the room looking for what, I didn't know, but with her it could be anything. She was admired as being one of the finest investigators in the Department and she knew exactly what needed to be found to close a case.

"Hey, come check this out," Riley said, motioning for us to join her. As I started toward Riley, I glanced at Nana who was going out the door. I'd seen that look on her face many times before…she was thinking and didn't want to be distracted. Waving it off I made my way to where Riley crouched, "What'd you find?"

Riley pointed to some black goo approximately two inches long on the baseboard under the spot where the stolen painting used to be. "It might not be anything, but I'm going to take a sample and a photo. I'll look at it more closely later." Riley began rummaging through her backpack. She kept literally everything in that backpack. She pulled out some tweezers, a Ziploc bag, and a pair of rubber gloves.

"Sounds like a plan," I said, bending over to get a better look, "kind of looks like it came from the sole of a black shoe, doesn't it?"

Riley tilted her head and looked up at me, "No," she said. "Not the black mark, the goo in the crevice above it." Goo? What goo? I thought squatting down to get an even closer look. Riley stood up and started snapping more photos of the entire area as Nana strolled toward us.

"Anything," I asked standing up.

"Yep, I checked all the entrances and exits, and this place cannot be entered without either keys or someone on the inside. Me, I'm thinking both."

So, it's definitely an inside job. "Ok," I said. "Then we now have nine possible suspects, right?"

"It sure looks that way," Nana said.

"I think it's time we had another sit down with Angela Gates," I suggested. Riley opted to stay behind to take more photos and look around.

We made our way down the stairs and noticed Brynn was nowhere to be found, so we walked down the corridor to Angela's office. As we approached, we could hear her voice through the slightly open door. I held my hand up, signaling a stop.

"I understand, yes," Angela said, "I *said* I'll handle it."

I glanced back at Nana. She nodded, the same thought crossed both our minds. Handle what? I walked to the door, poked my head inside and gently knocked. When she saw me, she quickly said, "I'll take care of it, I have to go." She quickly hung up the phone. I haven't been on many conference calls, but that didn't sound like one.

Nana whispered behind me, "Oh yeah! We're putting her at the top of the suspect list." I gave her a gentle punch telling her she needed to zip it!

Angela motioned for us to enter. "How can I help you?"

"We're sorry to bother you again, but we have a few more questions," I said. She leaned casually back in her chair and sighed as if to say this is getting old. She had just a bit too much attitude when she wasn't talking to invisible people. "Do all of your employees have keys to the museum?"

"Yes, except the Janitor," she said.

"Has anyone reported their keys missing or misplaced for any length of time?" She leaned forward in her chair, staring at me. She

24

looked like a robot who had been programmed to answer the questions asked with simple, to-the-point answers.

"Not to me," she replied, stone-faced.

I was beginning to get very irritated with this one who was already on my radar for her funny shenanigans earlier. Nana quickly picked up on my agitation and took over. "Can we speak to the security guard on duty last Thursday?" I knew Nana was, like me, looking more for a reaction than the answer.

Angela stiffened like a corpse. Hit a nerve, have we? Knowing that the security guard working last Thursday was Walter Mayhew and Mike Irwin would be on duty today, I said, "Ms. Lewis told us we could speak to Mike Irwin."

"Yes, um," she said, relaxing slightly, "Mike has already arrived for his shift."

We thanked her once again for her time and headed out to find Mike Irwin. As we entered the main hall, we saw Riley standing in front of the souvenir shop speaking to a uniformed man about six feet with ash blonde hair that looked to be in his early thirties. Riley was writing something on a pad as we approached.

Looking up, Riley said, "Here they are," she obviously had informed him who we were and where we worked. "This is Mike Irwin. He is one of three security guards that work for the museum."

Mike shook both our hands as Riley continued the introductions, "Mike, this is Stephi Cay, and Raylan Lane." Riley continued, "I ran into Mr. Irwin while waiting for you. He has some interesting information I think you'll want to hear." Riley motioned for him to start. I smiled, sometimes forgetting that she was so young.

"I was just telling the young lady that my shift ended at 3:00 pm. The closing security guard was Walter Mayhew." Nana and I looked at each other.

"Is Mayhew working today?" I asked glancing over at Riley who had her 'wait for it' smile ready.

I looked back at Mike as he said, "I haven't seen Walter Mayhew since my shift ended last Thursday."

Well, well now. Why hadn't Angela shared this bit of information with us? If he was nowhere to be found, that made him a prime suspect. And what was Angela's role in all this? And what did she need to 'handle'? "Just a few more questions, Mr. Irwin. Do the security officers sign in and out for their shifts, or maybe a time clock?"

Mike pointed to the concierge desk and said, "We check in with Brynn, who has our sign-in sheet." At this bit of information, I watched as Nana walked over to the concierge desk and noticed Brynn still wasn't at her usual post, another employee had taken her place. I turned my attention back to Mike. "Did you notice anything unusual about Mr. Mayhew on Thursday?"

"Not really, but we didn't talk a lot either. He kept to himself most of the time. But" he offered, "you might want to talk to Brynn, she's engaged to him."

Oh, I am so loving this guy right now!

"So, has Ms. Lewis left for the day?" I asked as Nana joined us.

"I was told she had to take care of some personal business and wouldn't be back today," Mike offered.

"Just one last question. Exactly what painting was stolen?" Once again, the answer was the same, only without the near nervous breakdown.

We thanked him for his time and headed for the car. We needed to get back to the office. Even though Walter Mayhew was now our main suspect, I knew there was something else going on. As we made our way to the car, Nana informed us that the lady covering for Brynn was Kay Jones, one of the conservators for the museum. She had called in sick the day of the theft, her alibi...her husband. We also noticed that Mr. Avery's limousine was gone.

Before we could get through the office door, the phone began to ring. Nana was closest and snatched it up. Riley said she was going to upload the photo and analyze the piece of unknown substance she scraped off the wall. I went to my desk and pulled out the list of employees. I checked off the few employees that had possible alibis until I came to Walter Mayhew. Since all I had were names, I would have to do some extensive research for addresses. There were several matches with the name Walter Mayhew, but only one that lived in Springfield. I typed in Brynn Lewis's name, which yielded the same results. It seems Mike had been telling the truth about the two of them.

Time to do a little snooping. I grabbed my keys and said, "Guys, I'm going to pay a visit to the Mayhew house. See what I---."

"Mom, wait!" Riley interrupted. "You both might want to take a look at this."

Intrigued, we immediately made our way to Riley. It was one of the photos she had taken at the museum. "Tell me what you see," she said, looking at me.

I pointed out several of the obvious, the empty spot where the painting used to hang, the "do not cross" tape surrounding the area, and obviously the black mark.

Riley shook her head and looked at Nana, who stood there in a daze. It was clear she only saw the same things I did. "Geez, if you two didn't already own glasses, I'd tell you to invest in some." Turning back to the computer screen she highlighted an area on the right side of the photo. "Do you see anything now?"

I moved in for a closer look, in the top right-hand corner was an image of what looked to be a face looking down on us as we investigated. There was no way this could be a person. It was too high and there was nowhere for a human being too stand. I looked at Riley. "Um, Riles. Are you suggesting there is a ghost in the museum?"

Behind me, I could feel Nana shake her head as she always did when the subject of ghosts came up, *"there are no such thing as ghosts,"* she would always say. She didn't believe in ghosts but when it came to the subject of aliens, she could talk indefinitely. *"we're ignorant if we think we are the only living things in the universe,"* was her response to my thoughts on aliens and their existence. I did believe in aliens, but she didn't have to know that.

Riley and I, on the other hand, were firm believers in ghosts. We'd even gone on a few ghost hunts with Steve, a friend from college, who now did local ghost hunting full time. But, to say a ghost stole a painting, *that* I couldn't wrap my head around. Which I voiced to my daughter. "I don't know Riles, seems a little farfetched. I mean, we have a possible suspect in Walter Mayhew and then there's the black marks…."

"I agree it sounds farfetched, but it's a possibility. At least something to investigate."

"Okay, look, I'll give Steve a call and see if he knows of any reported activity in or around the building." With that decided, Riley smiled and continued looking through the photos.

"Well, I'm sticking to real evidence," Nana said. "That was Doug on the phone, he got us a copy of the security tape. It should tell us for sure what happened to the painting. I'll head to the police station while you call your…ghost friend…" she said waving her hand at me.

I rolled my eyes at her back as she hurried through the front door. Although I trusted Riley's instincts, I still wanted to check out Mayhew's house. Something just didn't feel right about that whole situation.

I really wanted Riley to look at that security tape and analyze it. "I've got my cell on ring, let me know if you find anything." Now, I'm really bad about putting my cell phone on vibrate and not checking it. Yes, this is not a good habit when you have a seventeen-year-old, but Riley knows the protocol if I don't answer…call Nana. Which she does anyway before calling me.

"Mom," Riley said then paused, "be careful. We don't know what we're up against yet." After the death of her father, Riley became overly protective of me. As did I with her. We looked out for each other.

I nodded with understanding, "Love you." She gave me the heart sign with her hands, I returned the gesture.

Chapter Four

I had just strapped on my seatbelt when my phone started ringing. The screen let me know it was Steve. Bill and Steve had been best buds in college and that friendship had lasted until Bill's death. I chuckled remembering the time Steve told me 'Bill better watch out, he's gonna turn around and I'll snatch you up.' I would laugh and gently punch him in the arm. When Bill died, he was devastated, and he had promised Bill he would take care of us. Which he upheld to a tee and come to think of it, probably why he got us hooked on ghost hunting to keep our minds busy. His knowledge of the paranormal was amazing and although he had a decent following everyone in the Springfield and surrounding areas knew he was the go-to person for any kind of paranormal phenomenon. I clicked the answer button, "Steve, what's up?"

I should've known the next words to come out of his mouth would be a smart-aleck reply. "Uh, the sky!"

"Ha-Ha. You're in a good mood, catch some gnarly ghosts last night?"

"No, unfortunately." His jovial tone turned sour. "Our former client thought it would be funny to rig some mirrors, sheet ghost, and other crap to see if we would fall for it. Pissed me off he wasted our time just to make fun of our work." Steve was serious about his work and didn't take kindly to being mocked. In his jovial voice again, "However, he won't be so happy when he receives my hefty bill."

I laughed. "Don't take it too personal, we've been on several jobs with you and the gang, we know what's out there. You've done a lot of great work helping people. You and your team have the respect of the city." He replied with a thanks which prompted me to change the subject. "So, did you talk to Riley? She seems to think there is paranormal activity in the museum. What's your take on it?"

"Yeah, she filled me in on the situation. Unfortunately, nothing has come through our office about paranormal activity at the museum. So, I can't make any assessments until I've seen what Riles found and had a look at the crime scene. It's an old building so it's possible there could be *something* paranormal. You know I never rule it out unless I can debunk it. And there have been instances where spirits have haunted objects, so it's not totally out in left field."

"Can you have your team find out about the building and the portrait? I'm going to dig deeper into the Avery family past. See if I can find out about this mysterious daughter no one knows about." I told him who to contact at the museum and if he needed anything to call me. Steve said he would get everyone on it ASAP and we said our goodbyes.

The drive to Walter's house took all of about ten minutes so I had to put the paranormal on the back burner for now. Walter lived in an older neighborhood that had seen its fair share of flooding before Springfield city council decided to put in retention ponds. As I drove down the street, my head bounced back and forth like I was watching a tennis match as I scanned the addresses on each house. When I found the right address the house looked worn from lack of upkeep. It was a Craftsman-style bungalow, built sometime between 1905 and 1930, if memory served. I had learned all about the different styles of homes from my mother. As I turned into the driveway, I noticed two cars parked in front of a two-car garage. Funny two cars were here, wouldn't Walter have been driving his? I put my Mustang in park and headed up the concrete walkway to the front door. After a few knocks, I wasn't surprised to see Brynn Lewis on the other side. She, on the other hand, looked once more like she had seen a ghost when she saw me.

"Hi," I said, with a smile.

"Oh, Ms. Cay," she said, nervously. "What brings you here?"

"I just have a few questions to ask you," I said. "May I come in?"

She hesitated, then reluctantly moved from the door frame so I could enter. The inside of the house also needed some TLC but was remarkably well-kept. Stepping further inside, I was immediately met with a living room. Off to the left was the kitchen and a breakfast nook. To my right, a hallway led to what I assumed were some bedrooms and a bathroom. If you walked directly through the living room, there were two sliding glass doors leading to an enclosed patio. "You have a lovely home," I said.

A thank you was her only reply. "I was told at the museum that you had left for personal reasons. I apologize for any inconvenience I might be causing."

"It's fine, really," she said, but I knew she didn't mean it. She motioned toward the sectional couch. "Would you like some tea, coffee…?"

I thanked her but declined. I wasn't here for social hour. "I was told you and Walter Mayhew are engaged." With this comment came a flood of tears. I picked up the box of tissues on the coffee table and offered her one. From the pile of tissues, it was obvious she had come home because she was upset about something, and that something probably had to do with Walter.

32

She nodded thanks, wiped her eyes and with a shaky voice said, "Y-yes, we were planning to be married in November this year. It was going to be a huge wedding, with…with…" A new wave of tears followed. I sat there patiently waiting for her to compose herself.

After several moments, she continued, "No one has seen him since his shift ended last Thursday." It was obvious she was heartbroken over his sudden departure, which is probably why she's been acting strange.

"I noticed you have two cars. Is one of them Walter's?"

She nodded and blew her nose, then said, "See, that's the strange thing, Ms. Cay. Besides his car, all his clothes are still here, his toiletries, suitcase…. everything! Why would he just take off and leave everything behind?" As another round of crying started, I began to wonder the same thing myself. "Didn't Walter take his car to work last Thursday?"

She sniffed and thought for a moment, "Um, yes," she blew her nose. "We usually rode to work together, but that day he said he picked up an extra job and would be home late." She started crying, and said, "If only I had…" She let the sentence trail off.

"If only you had what, Brynn?" She shook her head and waved off answering. "Well, then can you tell me what his extra job was?"

"All he would tell me is that he was doing a favor for a friend."

"Do you know the friend's name?"

"I asked him, but he just said, 'you wouldn't know him'. But I knew all of his friends!" And the tears flooded out again.

Okay, the friend was a him, so that was start. And if Brynn knew all of Walter's friends, then he was working for someone other than a friend. "Do you mind if I take a look around?" She nodded while blowing her nose.

I decided to start with the unknown down the hallway. My initial assumption was correct. There were two bedrooms on the left, one on the right. Straight ahead at the end of the hall a bathroom door was partially ajar. As I entered the first room there were two big windows with blinds that looked out onto the enclosed patio. I checked for any signs of a break-in.....nothing. Underneath the windows sat one of those two-sided adjustable beds. On the far back wall were two doors, one led to a small bathroom, the other a walk-in closet. I checked the bathroom first and just as Brynn had said, all his toiletries still sat around the sink area. Behind the bathroom door was sort of linen closet with some towels, washcloths, and more toiletries. I exited the bathroom to check the closet. As I walked into the closet I felt something brush past my face. A light switch? I reached up, grabbed the unidentified object and pulled. A bright light lit up the area. On the left side were all Brynn's clothes and on the right were Walter's. All were in symmetry, light to dark colors, short too long. All their shoes were neatly lined along the closet floor. Pfft! You'd *never* see my closet like this! On the back wall of the closet were three built-in boxed shelves. I sifted through each one taking a mental note of the items, except for one. A Museum ID case. I opened it up and staring back at me was a white male about twenty-five, black hair and medium-light skin. Walter Mayhew. So that's what you look like.

I heard a noise behind me and turned. It was Brynn. "I'm sorry Ms. Cay, but I need to run an errand."

"Not a problem," I said, then asked, "Do you mind if I borrow Walter's ID?"

"Of course not," she said, her eyes still swollen and red from crying. I felt sorry for her. I wanted to comfort her, tell her everything would be okay. But it wouldn't be honest, because at this moment, I really wasn't sure if everything would be okay.

I thanked her and headed out to my car. To have your fiancé just vanish off the face of the earth. No note, text, phone call…nothing. I knew all too well the feeling of losing a loved one. It was devastating, and hard to rebound from. As I drove back to the office, I couldn't help but think of my husband Bill. I was lucky to have found him, he was a great father, and husband. And how he spoiled Riley and me. I smiled, remembering the time Riley, who was a huge comic book nerd (don't judge me, she gave herself this title), found out some actors from her movies would be at the big comic convention in Houston. Even though we both worked and lived paycheck to paycheck, Bill would work extra hours to make sure he had enough money so she could get autographs and photo ops with all of them.

My cell phone ringing startled me out of my trance. Yes, I actually answered it. Nana would be happy, especially since it was her calling.

"Hey Ma," I said keeping my eyes on the road.

"Riley wants to know if you're on your way back?" she said. I could hear Riley in the background stressing me to hurry.

"Be there in a few. What's up?" I asked curiously.

"We'll fill you in when you get here."

When I arrived at the office Riley was in her usual spot behind the computer, Ma was hanging up the phone as I entered. "Finally! What took you so long? I called you thirty minutes ago" I looked at her like she was nuts. I had literally just spoken with her ten minutes ago.

"While you were at the Lewis house, Nana went to the station and got the security tape." She was telling me stuff I already knew. I waved my hand in a circular motion, indicating to get on with it and tell me something I *didn't* know. Riley waved me over and being an obedient mother, I complied. I stood behind Riley as she said, "Okay, the curator lady, what's her name...Gates? She said there were eight security cameras, right? We both nodded. "They are using the best cameras on the market right now. There isn't an inch of that room not covered."

"So..." I said waiting for more. Which I knew there would be...there always was.

"So," she repeated, "there can only be one explanation...the tape was on a loop. Someone had to have tampered with it. Here, I'll show you." Riley started the tape, which showed eight angles of the museum room. She clicked on the upper right screen, then clicked another button so the video moved slowly. I noticed the time stamp on the video showed seven twenty-two. Riley had gone through most of it since arriving back at the office, so we were starting at the spot where she found the glitch.

As we watched, nothing seemed out of the ordinary. People came, people left. One of the security guards, Mike Irwin, came into view. He circled the room, then left. A few minutes later Walter Mayhew entered, circled half the room, then stopped in front of the stolen painting, which also gave us a face to the mysterious Avery

36

daughter. Then at the precise moment, the picture flickered ever so slightly. "Stop," I said vehemently. Riley clicked to pause the video, then turned to me and said, "You saw it, right?"

I nodded, pointing to the monitor. "Right here, while Mayhew is standing in front of the painting. For a split second, it looks like he turned, but he didn't."

"Right," Riley said. "Someone tampered with the cameras, but who?"

"I'll call Ms. Gates and see who has access to the cameras," Nana said returning to her desk.

"Good catch, baby girl," I said.

Riley swiveled around to face me. "What did you find at the Mayhew house?" Before I could share my info Nana walked back over.

"Seems the only person in charge of the monitors is…drumroll…," we all said it in unison. Angela Gates. It seems my initial intuition about Angela was spot on. This woman was involved somehow, and I would be looking deeper into her background.

"This is what I think," Nana began, "When Mayhew stopped in front of the painting that's when Angela started the loop. The time on the video proves she was still there at that time. Maybe she was working with Mayhew?"

"That's a good deduction," I said. But Riley's findings in her photo crept back into my mind. "Riles, do you have a camera angle that matches the photo you took earlier? The one with the face."

Riley swiveled back to her screen and started skimming through the video. While Riley continued her search, I looked over at Nana.

"If Walter and Angela *are* in cahoots, we need something concrete to connect the two."

"Well, let's start with what you found out at the Mayhew house," Nana said.

As Riley continued to scour over the video, I filled them both in on my little excursion to Walter Mayhew's house and showed them the ID. I told them I didn't think Brynn was involved; her tears of heartache were genuine. I knew that from experience. But I did suspect she knew more than she was saying by her actions when I arrived. And the fact that she suddenly had an errand to run. And what was this girl so scared of?

Chapter Five

As we sat grueling over information at our desks a loud clap of thunder and bright lightning scared the bejesus out of us. We looked out the front window. The rain coming down made it look like eight o'clock at night instead of six and the wind was blowing so hard it sounded like a howling wolf. I checked my cell, which was exploding with Weather alerts. Where the heck is all this coming from? A quick look at the radar on my weather app showed a low coming from the northwest merging with a high coming from the south. My sinuses were *definitely* equipped with radar.

"Looks like we'll be investigating indoors today, ladies," I said. They both ignored my obvious assumption. One thing you learn from growing up in this area, when you have flash flood rain…you stay put! Too many deaths occur when people try to go through high water. And this was *definitely* flash flood weather.

I looked over at Riley who had already gone back to skimming through the videos. The thunder might have surprised her at first, but she was used to Texas weather being erratic and calmly went back to analyzing the mark on the wall she found earlier. I glanced over at Nana, who also had gone back to work looking for a connection between Mayhew and Gates.

I went the other direction scouring through article after article on Mr. Avery's mysterious daughter. I tried Google, entering everything I could think of but nothing about a daughter existed, at least not in the media. Several articles came up on the Avery's, of course. Parties, humanitarian awards, and grand openings he attended. There were a few scandals splashed in there as well. One in particular caught my eye, remembering it as if it happened yesterday. There might not be anything in the media on a daughter, but everyone in town knew of his son, Matthew Avery or Matty as we liked to call him in high school only because he hated it. Just like his father he was extremely handsome. He had his father's money and he used it to get what he wanted, mainly the girls in school. They naturally flocked to him like bees to honey but it only took one getting pregnant to bring the Avery house to shame. Mr. Avery and his wife tried to keep it all hush hush and to this day no one knows how it leaked out. But it did and the media loved it. Matty was forced to marry her, which didn't last long with his adulterous ways. Last I heard, through gossip, she and the child were living quite nicely off Mr. Avery's money in a different state. As for Matty, nothing came up on his current whereabouts.

"Did you find anything?"

Startled, I looked away from the computer screen to find Nana looking at me impatiently. "Huh?" was all I could get out.

"I've asked you the same question three times," she said now getting even more irritated.

"Sorry. No, I haven't found anything on the daughter yet, but I haven't searched the vital statistics records." She nodded. "Did you find anything to connect Angela and Walter?"

She started relaying the information she had found so far. Several articles popped up. She chose the wiki article first, since it would have a quick list of her life and work, awards, etc. The article stated she has a B.A. in Art History from the University of Houston, worked as research assistant while in graduate school and was a curatorial intern in New York. Probably where she met Mr. Avery. The article listed several awards, one of which she was voted one of the most influential people in America. Surely, he wouldn't hire someone with these credentials if she were shady, would he?

As if she had read my mind, Nana said, "The interesting part is she wasn't hired by Joseph Avery. She was hired by Matthew Avery."

Really, now that is *very* interesting. "Why would Matty be hiring for his dad's museum?" I said, pausing before continuing. "I think we need to add Matthew Avery to our list of possible suspects."

"Why? I haven't heard anything about that boy in, oh what ten years. Pretty sure he's been locked away for knocking up too many women."

"Ma!" I said chuckling. "We don't judge, remember. Maybe he turned over a new leaf?" She looked at me as if to say 'Pfft, not that one.' I knew however, she could be right. Our junior year Matty had made friends with some bad kids at school. Across the street from the school was the Snack Shack, an abandon rundown old house the bad kids would use to hang out. Being the child of a police officer and mainly fear of getting my ass whooped by my mom, I never darkened that door. Rumors flowed through school that unlawful things went on over there, mainly drugs and weed being sold and used. Now back then, Springfield was a small town, so the rumors were like ninety-nine-point-nine percent true. And rumors spread fast! Mr. Avery found out Matty was a regular at the Snack Shack and threatened to send him to military school if he didn't straighten up. Which, of course, never came to pass. Matty just made his indiscretions more subtle. "Well," I suggested, "why don't you see what you can find on Matty. See how he's doing." Nana raised an eyebrow, and I knew that look was her telling me to get back to my business and she would handle hers. Sheesh, she was so sensitive sometimes.

As I began typing in the URL for Vital Statistics, the phone rang. I looked at Ma and Riley, who were so engrossed in their work, they didn't hear or more likely chose not to answer. Guess it was my turn. I picked up the phone and before I could get out my usual professional spiel, a frantic voice on the other line cut me off.

"Thank God you're there, Ms. Cay!"

The voice sounded familiar, and I took a wild guess. "Brynn?" I asked. At this, Ma and Riley looked up from their work.

"Can you help me, please. Please!" She started crying and her words became slurred and erratic.

"Brynn," I said calmly, "take a deep breath and tell me where you are." I could hear the deep breath, her words were clearer, but still frantic.

"I'm scared, Ms. Cay. Please…help me!"

"Brynn, *where* are you?" I pressed.

"I-In Walter's car…someone's in the house…" she said as the connection died.

I slammed down the phone and grabbed my keys. Nana and Riley both belted out 'What?' I told them something was wrong at Brynn's house, and I needed to get over there pronto.

"Oh, hell no," Nana stated adamantly. "I'm going too."

"Well, you two are NOT going without me." Riley chimed in.

"Fine," I said without any fuss. Normally, I handled the crazy stuff while Nana would stay back with Riley. It was an agreement we had after Bill's passing to ensure Riley was taken care of. Only one of us would be in harm's way at any given time. This time I had a gut feeling I would need both of them.

The rain was nothing but a sprinkle now as I drove fast, but safely to Brynn's. I didn't know what to expect when I arrived, but I was armed and had been trained by the best…my mom. I had also picked up a few little techniques from Dougie, which Nana didn't know about. I parked on the opposite side of the street and scanned the house. Brynn's car still sat in the same place and there was no visible movement outside of the house. The garage door was now closed, so I wasn't sure if Walter's car was inside or gone. Both cars had been in the driveway when I was here earlier. Turning to face them I said, "Ok, here's the plan. I'll go clear the house. If I'm not back in ten minutes," this time looking straight at Nana, "Call Dougie."

Flipping the safety off my Colt, I stealthily made my way closer to the house using the tall evergreen shrubs along the right side of the driveway for cover. I noticed a door on the side of the garage and, keeping my eyes on the house, headed toward it. Out of the corner of my eye, I saw movement on the opposite side of the yard. I froze behind one of the tall bushes, gun ready and peeked around. The owner of the house next door was walking toward the curb with a garbage bag in each hand. Okay. Good. Not a threat. I turned and made my way to the garage door and cautiously glanced through the tic-tac-toe window. Walter's car was now inside the garage, and I could just make out the outline of a figure sitting in the driver's seat. I scanned the rest of the garage, well what I could see of it, before reaching for the doorknob. Damn. Locked. Okay, I'll have to go through the house. I headed for the house, checking before rounding each corner until I came to the front door. My back against the house, I tried the doorknob and was surprised to find it unlocked. I slipped in, clearing each room before heading for the door leading to the garage. Peeking around the door, I made one more sweep of the garage yielding nothing, except for one thing. What the hell! The figure in the car I had seen not more than two minutes earlier was gone. I checked every inch of the garage. Nothing. Holstering my gun, I opened the garage door and signaled all clear to Nana and Riley.

"Did you find her?" Riley asked as they both walked toward the garage. I told them the house was clear and about the figure I had seen in the car that had mysteriously vanished when entering the garage. "Are you sure it was Brynn?"

"Well, no." I tried to imagine the figure more clearly but the dirty film on the window wouldn't allow it. "But who else could it have been? She told me she was in Walter's car."

The look in Riley's eyes told me her brain was fast at work. Moving toward the car, she started searching the inside of the vehicle. I followed suit. Something happened in the car that we were sure of. Ma decided to take her detective skills inside the house, since Brynn said someone had been inside.

Riley took the driver's seat and I the passenger. I opened the glove compartment only to find the car manual and, I squinted closer at a dark object under some papers. Was that a half-eaten Heath bar? Ugh! Gross! Not only did I not like chocolate bars, but I really despised melted, half-eaten Heath bars. Nothing against the chocolate bar itself, I ate them as a child. Until. I closed off the unpleasant childhood memory that tried to creep from the depths inside me. I quickly closed the glove compartment. "Did you find anything?"

"Nothing," Riley said slumping back in the seat looking defeated. "I don't understand it, there's ab—"

When she stopped mid-sentence, I looked over at her. "Don't understand what?" The look on her face was whiter than a sheet. "What is it, Riles? Are you okay? Riley, say something!" She was beginning to scare me when suddenly she snapped out of her trance and pointed at the rearview mirror. Not in a position to see into the mirror, I turned and nearly crapped my pants.

Sitting in the middle of the back seat was a young girl, about six years old dressed in a pink fluffy dress with a pink bow in her hair. She had light brown hair and beautiful emerald-green eyes. If it hadn't been for the fact that I could see the vinyl seat through her I would swear she was real. She looked at me with a yearning that could have said 'Help me'. Mesmerized, I sat there frozen by what I was seeing. Was I really seeing a ghost? I willed my eyes to close, thinking when I opened them the figure would be gone. I opened my eyes. Not only was the apparition still there, she began to reach for me. At that moment Nana came bursting into the garage and poof just like that, the girl was gone.

I sat there still staring at the space the ghost had occupied. I felt a hand touch my arm. I jump, but realized it was Riley. I slowly turned around, taking a minute to regain my senses. "What the hell just happened?" I asked Riley afraid to take my eyes off the front of the garage, and who apparently was also coming out of her own trance. "Did we just see…"

Shaking her head, she managed to get out, "Yep." We slowly looked at each other and smiles crept onto our faces. Jumping out of the car we went literally nuts! Between the shouts of 'this is crazy' and 'it looked so real' I started dialing Steve's number, he needed to get over here pronto!

"Uh, Hello." Nana's voice boomed at us. She really didn't have much choice; we were still screaming.

Riley told Nana what had happened and finally, after several times punching in Steve's phone number, I finally got it right. Hey, I was excited. Never have we actually seen a ghost. In all our investigations with Steve, it's only been knocks, footsteps and things being tossed about. This was an actual *ghost*! Damn! I thought as I waited for his voicemail. I explained what happened and for him to get back with me ASAP!

"Hold the phone!" Riley said, and I looked at the phone I was holding. She rolled her eyes and waved at my hand. "If we saw the ghost here, then what Steve said about ghosts attaching itself to an object could be a possibility, right?"

"Right," I said pocketing my phone. "Which means the painting must be here at the house."

"This is ridiculous," Nana said, still not convinced we actually saw a ghost. Then the cop in her reared its ugly face and she smiled, "I can't let you just go into someone's house and starting nosing around without a warrant. I taught you better than that didn't I?" Then in a snarky voice, "Oh. yeah. I know I did."

Riley and I looked at each other. She was right and like we were going to tell the police we saw a ghost. Of course, Dougie would believe us, but no one else would. Not everyone believes in ghosts, which is fine, not everybody does. But right now, I *really* needed Steve to call back. And, of course, what would be fantastic would be to find Brynn and Walter.

"Okay, you're right," I conceded. "We'll go through the proper channels." My mind began to churn as I closed the garage door, and we made our way back to the car. We could let the police do their due diligence here until we got an all-clear. Then I would get in touch with Steve about coming here and conducting an investigation. Riley and I *know* what we saw, and it was definitely an apparition no matter what Nana thought. Now as to who it could be, why they were here and what they wanted was a whole different ball game. I knew it had to be old Avery's daughter, but why was she here at Brynn's house? And where were Brynn and Walter? Did she scare them, and they bolted? As we climbed into the car, I started to share my deduction with Nana and Riley, but I was beaten to the punch.

"I know the painting is in there," Riley began, "And I know the ghost is attached to it." She paused. I was about to ask her how she knew this when a slight whimper floated from the back seat where Riley sat. Nana and I slowly turned in our seats. Me, a bit slower, after what I had just seen I was a little cautious of back seats now.. Relief spread over me; it was just Riley in the back seat. Or so I thought. Her hands in her lap and her head hung low. The whimpering changed to crying. Riley wasn't the crying type not after Bill passed away. She cried for a solid week leading up to his death. Then, not a single tear slid from her eyes. At the time I thought she had cried herself out, but later she confessed that she had a dream that Bill had come to her and told her everything would be all right and he would always be with them watching over them. This was a comfort, even if it was a dream.

"Riley?" She slowly raised her head. Her eyes damp from the crying she looked directly at me. Her expression was pleading as she reached toward me. I just stared at her, unable to speak. Then…

"Help me."

Then as quickly as it had started, Riley blinked and looked at both of us. The vacant stare that once donned her face how now been replaced with confusion. "What? Why are you looking at me like that?" she asked wiping the tears from her face. "And why am I crying?"

Chapter Six

After a long night of reassuring Riley she was still not possessed, I let her sleep in. It was a school day, but she never missed, so I figured she was due, especially after last night. Riley is a very level-headed, strong-willed girl and for her to break down like that had me worried. My first call this morning would be to Steve. He was the expert on this. I just tagged along on his investigations for fun. But this was way beyond my area of expertise. I started to dial his number when my phone started ringing. The screen told me it was Steve. Probably calling back from yesterday.

"Hey, Steve." There was no pep in my voice, which he picked up on immediately. After last night, I was still too sleepy.

"Hey," he said hesitantly, obviously picking up on my tone. "You, okay?"

"Um, let me think. No." I half-assed told Steve what had happened. Afterwards exhaustion hit me like a brick wall. And when that happens, there's only one way I go...I started bawling like a baby.

"I'm leaving now, and I'll bring Celeste. If anything is amiss, she'll know." I knew Celeste from the investigations we went on. Her ability to communicate with spirits was amazing. Surely, she could tell us what the spirit wanted. And why was it speaking through Riley? Why not me or Nana? Okay, no one would want to get into Nana's mind, not even a spirit. Ever since her father's death, I've noticed Riley has been really in tune with things. Sometimes knowing when things would happen before they did. At the time I didn't think anything of it, but now, my mind was reeling with possible scenarios.

By the time Steve and Celeste arrived, I had regained my wits. I met them on the porch, still not sure if Riley was ready to relive the event again. "Hey guys," I said as they walked up the porch steps.

"Well, you sound a lot better than you did twenty minutes ago." Steve pointed out as he made his way toward me. Steve was as handsome as the first day I layed eyes on him. He was tall, lean, with dirty blonde hair and eyes bluer than mine, but you couldn't take him to the beach, his fair skin would burn in seconds. He put his hand on my arm a guided me over to the table and chairs that sat strategically on the front porch to catch the evening breeze. As I began elaborating on the events that happened, Nana joined us with some iced tea. I looked at her, she nodded knowing I wanted to know about Riley. I relayed the events that happened after we left the house and seeing the apparition.

"Has Riley had blackouts before?" Celeste asked. Celeste wasn't just beautiful, she was ethereal. Her tanned skin was as smooth as a baby's bottom and I secretly hoped when I reached her age, my skin would be the same. She always wore dark purple and black clothing donning so much jewelry you'd think she was rich. But it was her sweet, loving nature that drew people to her. Well, and her psychic ability.

"No," I looked over at Nana who shook her head in agreement with me." Well, we have never seen any." She pulled a pad from her jacket and scribbled something on it.

"Has she ever had visions that she couldn't explain? Dreams?" Again, my answer was no. Which wasn't completely true, Riley had a few dreams, but it was me who had the dreammare's. I wasn't ready to divulge that information yet. Again, she wrote something down. What the heck did she keep writing down. Did she already have a theory about Riley? Did she know I was fibbing?

"What are you writing down?" I finally asked her. "Do you know why she channeled a spirit?"

She looked from her pad to me. "I'm not certain, I would need to speak with Riley of course, but I think she might be sensitive to spirits."

Okay, didn't see that one coming. "Sensitive?" I knew Celeste was a psychic, but I never really asked her about what she did. Now, here she was telling me my daughter might be like her. I shook my head, "No…no…no! Riley is not like *you*!" As soon as the words spilled from my mouth, I wanted to take them back. "I'm sorry. I didn't mean being a psychic was bad."

As if she read my mind, which she probably did, she smiled and said, "It's okay, I understand." She put a hand on my arm. "I was new to this at one time too. I was scared, my parents were scared. Until we learned how to deal with it."

"But she's never shown signs of being 'sensitive' as you say. Hell, I don't even know what it means."

"There are different types of psychics out there. My abilities are more along the line of being able to use my senses to find spirits. Entering a room I can feel sadness, fear, happiness, etc. I believe Riley could be more of a medium for spirits." Seeing the confusion still stuck on my face, she continued. "A medium, on the other hand, has the ability to communicate between spirits and the living. There are three different types of mediumships or channeling. Séance

51

tables, trance, and Ouija. From what you have described, I'm almost positive Riley has this ability through trance."

Well, at least it wasn't a Ouija board. I hate those things and would never have or allow one in my home. I looked over at Nana who was dumbstruck. She wasn't sure what to believe. "So, what do we do next?"

"First, I need to speak with Riley. Alone." Celeste said adamantly. A look of shock must have covered my face because she raised her hand. "Only because in order to get an accurate reading, I cannot have any outside interference."

I looked over at Steve. I trusted him with my life, if he gave the go, I was in. Without hesitation, he shook his head in agreement. I shifted my gaze back to Celeste, "Okay…"

"Stephi," Nana said with obvious concern in her voice. "Are you sure about this?" I knew by her tone that this wasn't our usual playful arguments about whether ghosts were real or not. She was genuinely concerned but I needed to know. Riley had been through far worse than finding out she's a medium.

"Riley is stronger than you think." I said cutting my eyes at her, "She'll be okay." Nana jerked out of her chair, obviously pissed at my decision. But it was *my* decision. As she stomped upstairs, yes, the whole neighborhood could hear her going up the stairs, I turned to Celeste, "Why would this happen now? If she can channel spirits, wouldn't this have happened when Bill passed away? Wouldn't she have been able to see him?"

"Not necessarily. If a spirit had a violent death or died suddenly, they will stay because they have unfinished business." Her face turned to concern," If I may ask, how did your husband pass?"

"Bill was a Deputy Sheriff. He was shot during a domestic violence call." It was hard for me to talk about it, even now after five years. I still missed him. "He was in critical condition for a week. Then he started to get better, then just like that," I snapped my fingers, "he was gone. The doctors said it was an infection. How is that possible if you're on antibiotics." Steve knew I was on the verge of a breakdown and was at my side in an instant. "Fortunately, we were able to say our goodbyes before he passed away," I said, composing myself. Normally, I didn't have breakdowns, I was a rock. Unless the subject of Bill's death came up, coupled with the nightmares. Celeste voice brought me back to reality.

"Because you were able to say your goodbyes, he has moved on having made peace with God and with his family." There was an awkward silence before Celeste continued, "This spirit…of the little girl. Something must have happened to her if she is still here. She is trying to communicate through your daughter, but because Riley is inexperienced in using her abilities, the spirit just took over for that split second. I can help her understand and control her ability."

Before I could reply, Nana and Riley came through the screen door. I immediately made my way to Riley and hugged her. She held me tighter than a bear hug. I could hear a slight whimper as she buried her face in my shoulder. I never wanted to let her go, but I knew she needed help. I definitely could not help with this one. "How you doing baby girl?"

"I'm better, really." She pulled away from me, trying to be the strong one as always. She wiped her eyes and smiled. "Okay, so Nana tells me I'm into ghosts."

We all looked at each other. A smile creeped onto Riley face, and we all began to laugh. Now *that* was my baby girl. And now that things were semi normal again, Celeste said she would get back with us in a few days to start working with Riley. The team was working on a new case, and they should have it wrapped up soon. Steve said to let him know when the police finished their investigation and since the owners were nowhere to be found, maybe the police could give them permission to investigate.

Chapter Seven

The next morning, we were running late so the three of us piled into Nana's car and stopped at the local donut shop for kolaches before dropping Riley at school. It was like the previous day never took place. Except for getting up too late, it was business as usual. Riley was in unusually good spirits (no pun intended), Nana was her usual pain in the rear nagging about everything and me, well I'm still creeped out by it all. But I wasn't about to let either one of them see it.

The sun struggled to peek out from behind clouds, shedding some hope of a rainless day. Yesterday's torrential downpours had brought Houston and some surrounding areas to a standstill with flooding streets and freeway underpasses. The bayous and rivers were at their peak and any more rain like the day before would be even more devastating.

We arrived at the office to find a limo parked out front…across several parking spaces…are you kidding me? Mr. Avery had decided to grace us with his presence. Well, I don't care who he is, parking that way in front of *his* business was one thing, but this way *my* business and I wasn't going to have none of it! Ma and I looked at each other, thinking the same thing 'what the hell is he doing here.' I haven't even had my K-cup this morning! Unfortunately, I had to put my pissing mood in check and we both put on our professional faces when he came strolling through the door behind us.

"Mr. Avery," I said, extending my hand. "Welcome."

His voice was low and sultry but refined. "Ms. Cay," he shook my hand then extended his hand to Nana who looked at it and then at him. "Ms. Lane," he said withdrawing the gesture. Unharmed by Nana's snub, he sat down at my desk and started to look over the papers I had left out the day before.

I grinned at him and started gathering them into a pile. "How can we help you?"

"Might I bother you for a cup of coffee?" he asked, with a wicked blinding smile. How did he get his teeth so white? I walked to the Keurig as he continued, "I passed on my usual coffee this morning in hopes that I might share it with you two lovely ladies." Is he sucking up…Or just trying to be debonair? It was hard to tell. But I knew without seeing, Nana was rolling her eyes at that comment. I asked him how he took his coffee. Black was his response and then he went into a spiel about preservatives and how they weren't good for you. I handed him the mug and said, "That's all very fascinating Mr. Avery, but why are you here?" I was fed up with all of this sappy crap.

He took a sip of coffee and said, "I came by to get an update on the case. Mr. Pittman has informed me that you have not contacted him."

"It's only been one day," Nana said through clenched teeth. She was doing a great job keeping a lid on her temper…kudos Ma! There was a history with these two according to Nana who had shared stories of how she had butted heads with Mr. Avery when she was on the force. Especially when it came to his son Matty. Her cell phone buzzed, she snatched it up and seeing who the caller was, left the room.

"So, you had Mr. Pittman hire us, why?" I asked. Before he could reply I said, "The police are very capable of handling the case."

"Yes, of course they are. However, I need the matter investigated quickly and discretely." I felt the urge to bust out laughing…but suppressed it with a smile. Discretely. This from a man who drove around in a black stretch limo, had his driver park across several parking spaces so he wouldn't have to walk far, and whose family had co-founded Springfield. Everyone knew who they were…so there was no being discrete. The theft had been splattered all over the papers since Thursday.

He looked around me and looked at Nana through the doorway and then leaned closer to me and lowering his voice, "Ms. Cay, I know Raylan and I have had our differences in the past. However, I also know that she was and still is one of the best detectives in this city. As are you Ms. Cay." I nodded my gratitude. "I need you both to *find* this painting. It has special meaning to our family and losing it is far greater than any monetary value." There was an awkward silence.

When I finally found my voice, I asked, "This painting, is it a portrait of your daughter?" His reaction wasn't even close to what I expected. I figured he would freak out like the people at the museum.

He smiled, "And that's why I want you," he nodded toward Nana and took a sip of coffee before continuing, "and Raylan on this case. Your keen intuition is remarkable."

"Excuse me, but…and I don't mean to pry." I was trying to be respectful but, hell that's not me. "I grew up with your son, but I don't remember you having a daughter."

"No, you wouldn't," he said matter of factly. "Elizabeth was born many years after Matthew. She passed away when she was a young girl," he set the coffee cup on the desk. "The portrait was painted shortly before her death. It's been hanging in our home until recently, when I decided to put it in the museum."

Well, that explained why the painting was there and who it was, but why out of the blue would he want to put in the museum? And why would someone want to steal it? Did a secret hide within that portrait? Questions kept flooding my mind now that I knew who was in the painting.

"So," he said, interrupting my brain flood. "Have you found the painting yet?"

I filled him in on what we had so far, leaving out what had happened with the ghost. Which really wasn't keeping anything from him, the whole spirit thing was still unbelievable. So, instead I told him the fiancé of our prime suspect had been kidnapped yesterday and we were still looking into it. Or so we thought, we didn't know for sure, there was no proof yet of a kidnapping. We planned to go back to Walter's house and do a more thorough search, after the police finished their investigation and we were allowed back in. This seem to please him that we were already close to finding the culprit…which we weren't. We had no idea where Brynn and Walter were…. yet! He stressed keeping Mr. Pittman informed and thanked me.

Nana emerged from the other room just as the closed behind him. "Aw, man! Did I miss my friend leaving?" she said, sarcastically.

I laughed and shook my head. "Yes, you did." I took a sip of coffee. "Who was on the phone?"

"Doug. He said they were done at the Mayhew house."

"Great! Did they find anything?" I asked.

"Just fingerprints, which Doug said they would run through the system. But I suspect they belong to Brynn and Walter. He'll phone us when he knows for sure," she paused, and I glanced over at her as she sat down at her desk.

"What?"

"Well," she hesitated.

"What?!" I was losing patience now.

"Well, Doug did mention," she shook her head, "Ugh, I cannot believe I'm telling you this." She took a deep breath and exhaled heavily. "He said that the Mayhew house was a rental. If you want your ghostbuster buddies to investigate it, you have to contact the landlord to set it up." She handed me a piece of paper with the name and phone number of the owner of the house.

Although this was awesome news, it now meant, for this case anyway, we were adding paranormal investigation to our little P.I. business. Two days ago, Riley and I would've been pumped to go ghostbusting, but now I wasn't so sure especially now that she has superpowers.

"So what did dipshit want?"

I laughed, mainly because she had not used that word in so long I started to think she kept that specific word just for him and no one else. "Well, nothing really. However, I did get some info from him about the painting. He says it is a painting of his daughter who died when she was a child. Which would explain the little girl ghost we saw…" I let the sentence trail off.

"But?" Nana said knowing I wasn't finished.

"I don't believe him. I can't explain it, but I have a gut feeling he is lying."

Chapter Eight

We arrived at the school a little late, which was how our day seemed to be going so far, and had to listen to Riley complain about waiting and 'didn't I have a phone to check the time or text?' Why was everything my fault? Seriously, I never heard her blaming Nana for not watching the time. I slammed back with 'ever think about calling or texting me?' Then I got 'oh so you can *not* answer!' Nana raised her hand and growled, "Enough!" And that was the end of that. But I was still hyped. Too much had happened in the last twenty-four hours and I was still having trouble dealing with it. My baby girl, my sweet little Riles...a psychic! How does this happen out of the blue? Shouldn't there have been warning signs or something?

"Geez Riles," I said, in a lame attempt at an apology, "is something wrong? Did something happen at school?" She knew exactly what I was doing and spat back, 'Nothing!' When she got like that, I let her have space hoping she would come around.

We decided to grab some food on the way to the office. Nana began placing our order and was relaying Riley's when my cell phone rang. Riley kept changing her mind, so her and Nana kept going back and forth like a friggin' tennis match.

"Do you two *mind*!" I barked and they immediately ceased. I looked at Riley with a death stare and said through clinched teeth, "*Pick* something." Riley wasn't messing with that tone and obeyed. Nana apologized to the employee on the other end, and she instructed us to drive forward.

"Sorry Steve, food decisions are the worst," I said sarcastically while eyeballing them. As Steve began to talk, my demeanor became serious. I spouted out a lot of uh-huh's, okay's and really's before saying goodbye.

"What's up?" Riley asked, as the employee handed Nana our food. When I didn't answer, Riley looked at me. "Mom!"

"That was Steve," I said. They both shook their heads as if to say yes, we know that, tell us something we *don't know*! "Let's just say, Riley was right."

"Yes! I knew it!" she said excited. Then, "Wait, what was I right about?"

"Apparently, Mr. Avery's mother Margaret Elizabeth Avery became fascinated with the occult. Steve dug even deeper and after her husband died Margaret became so fascinated in the dark arts that she began using Ouija boards and holding seances in the hopes of bringing her dead husband back," I unwrapped my burger, took a hefty bite, chewed a few times and continued. "But here's the kicker, she also tried bringing her dead granddaughter back to the here and now. After the death of Elizabeth, Mr. Avery was so distraught he stayed in his room and never left the house for years. Margaret thought that if she couldn't bring her dead husband back, which she never accomplished or maybe she did, then maybe she could with little Lizzie and bring her back to Mr. Avery." Yes, I know but the last names don't match. Or do they? Steve said the girl was his *illegitimate* daughter. Naw, the geographics don't match. Amazing how my mind will wonder off course, "Steve said there have been cases where an object can be possessed by the spirit of its owner. This could be the case, especially with old Margaret dabbling in the occult and why we saw the face in the video, the weird experience Riley and I had at the Mayhew house. Plus, why the employees at the museum were acting weird." And on top of all that, I got that sign I asked for that Riles was a medium. Not only did she find evidence of the haunting, but she could feel it as well. Her reaction at first upset her, no doubt. But she's bounced back super quick. Makes me wonder if she's known about these "powers" for a while.

"How does Steve do that?" Nana asked, breaking my thoughts. "I've followed that family more closely than anyone during my entire career and none of that information was known. How did they keep stuff like that under wraps?"

I shrugged, "His team is the best. They can find things most people can't, especially paranormal." I knew that last bit would get at her, and I was right. Her eyes rolled so far into her eye sockets, it looked like she was being possessed by a demon. "Face it, you will just have to admit that spirits and ghosts are real and all around us."

She glanced at me, then at Riley who sat in the backseat. Her granddaughter's expression must have been tense, because she quietly said, "Maybe."

We reached the office a little after two. Steve had called on the drive back and let us know he got the okay from the landlord to investigate the house and asked if we wanted to join the hunt. I was sure Riley would say no, but she was more excited than I was. I looked over at Nana who adamantly shook her head no.

The investigation was set for the following night, so Nana and I decided to do what we do best and try to find what happened to Brynn and Walter. We were now not only working on a ghost investigation, but a missing person case. Plus, we still didn't know where the painting was. If Riley saw the little girl there, and she could possibly be haunting the painting then we needed to do a little searching of our own. While Steve and his team set up, we could look around. Maybe Riley could feel it or even better, the spirit could lead us to it. Celeste had text earlier and said she would be by the office today around three to start working with Riley. So here we were quietly working when…

"Mom, there's something I need to tell you," Riley said out of the blue. She glanced over at Nana, and I followed her gaze to look at my mother, trying to assess exactly what I was about to hear. I got nothing from either one of them.

I decided to keep it cool and calm. Leaning back in my chair, I asked, "What's up baby girl?"

She hesitated, looking first at me then back at Nana again. "Well, I haven't been *completely* honest with you." Okay, now I was getting curious.

"About?" I asked, letting the word trail off.

"The other day," she began, then hesitated. She was doing a lot of that. "Well, it wasn't the first time I've had an *'encounter'* with a spirit."

I looked over at Nana, then back at Riley. "Okay, when did it happen before?"

Again, she hesitated. Really, was she deliberately dragging it out for the drama effect? "Riley? When?" I asked calmly but knew what she was about to say.

She looked down at her hands that lay in her lap and whispered, "When dad died."

Goose bumps took over my entire body. I knew it! I knew she was about to tell me she'd seen Bill. I looked over at my mother who was staring at Riley with a look that said, 'are you sure'.

"It was at the hospital right after he passed away. He told me everything would be okay. That he loved us, and he'd always be with us."

"D-did you actually see him?" I managed to sputter out. She nodded yes. Oh my God, she actually saw him one last time. A rush of emotions swept over me at once. Jealousy, anger, sadness, happiness. What I wouldn't have given to see him even as a spirit one last time. I jumped up from my chair and began to pace, anger temporarily took over. I stopped in front of Riley. "Why didn't you tell me? Why would you keep something like that from me?"

"Mom, you were a mess! If I had told you what happened, you wouldn't have believed me. No matter how much you say you believe in spirits and ghosts." Riley stood up and put her arms around my waist. I pulled her close in a tight hug. "Believe me, I wanted to tell you," she whispered.

"I know baby girl, I know. It's okay, everything will be okay." I looked over at Nana. "I guess you knew already." She nodded.

"Nana said when the time was right, I'd be able to tell you."

"Well, for once I agree with her," I said with a grin. "But don't expect that will happen again." Our laughter and tears were interrupted when Celeste strolled through the door.

Chapter Nine

The next day was Saturday and ghost hunting day. The weather forecast promised thunderstorms and possible flash floods. Excellent weather for catching ghosts. Riley and I were up super early, bustling around the house excited about the upcoming investigation. Riley's session with Celeste went awesome, according to her. She was embracing her newfound ability. Which eased my mind...*a lot*! Now we could focus on the case and the investigation. Nana was already in the kitchen making breakfast. She might not be into ghostbusting, but she had always supported Riley and I on everything and today was no different. We were all sitting around the table, talking, and laughing. Just like normal. But our lives would never be normal again. Just like when Bill passed, we had to come together, changed our way of living. And, once again, we were okay with it. So starts another new chapter in the Lane-Cay family.

We were set to meet the gang at the house around four o'clock to help get the equipment ready. I told Riley about my plan to look around the house for the painting before starting the investigation. I still believed Riley when she said it was somewhere in the house. Why else would the ghost show herself there and not the museum? Or maybe it had and that's why the employees would freak out going into that part of the museum. I told Riley about my theory, and she assured me, for the umpteenth time, the painting was in the house somewhere and we would find it. Nana, of course, would not be attending feigning illness. We knew she was bugging out on us. Or is that ghosting out? Yet still, she was more open-minded about it now than she was before. But I knew it was for Riley's benefit.

We arrived at the house around three forty-five. Steve and the gang had already arrived and from previous ghost-hunting stints, we knew if the crew were waiting by the van it meant Steve, Celeste and Colton must be still inside with the owner. They were waiting for instructions on where they could set up the equipment inside the house. I parked behind the van which served as the command station. It held all the computers, monitors and equipment used in their investigations. They could monitor every room in the house in this one area. It was a pretty sweet setup. Steve said he got the idea from his favorite ghost-hunting duo. He had watched every season since the beginning, and he learned a lot just by watching the show. I remember the time he said, "Can you imagine what I could learn if I had the chance to investigate with them?" Which, in reality, he knew that would never happen, so he used the episodes like a learning video.

I looked over at Riley, a smile broke out on both our faces, and we sprang from the Mustang. We were headed toward the van when Steve emerged from the house followed by a man in what looked to be his early seventies, medium height and thin. But it was hard to tell, his skin was like crepe paper, tanned and worn, definitely from years of hard work. The two men were talking loudly and laughing, which wasn't surprising. Steve was friends with everyone. In college, if you wanted to know anything, he was the go-to guy. They stopped on the porch, continuing their conversation when Colton and Celeste emerged from the house. While Celeste was the resident psychic, it was Colton who headed up the tech crew. He would take notes on the initial walk-through so the crew would know where to set up the cameras. Upon seeing us, Celeste waved us over.

"Hey guys!" Riley and I said in unison, stopping at the foot of the stairs leading to the porch. She said out of the side of her mouth,

"Jinx." I ignored it knowing she would tell me what I owed her at a later time. But felt kind of honored since that was normally a thing only between her and Nana.

"Stephi, Riley!" Steve said in his normal bubbly self. He introduced us to the older man, whose name was George Wilson. Was that a coincidence? Hm, I guess he could be an elder version of the character George Wilson from Dennis the Menace.

I held out my hand, "Stephi Cay, it's nice to meet you Mr. Wilson. This is my daughter, Riley." I placed my hand on her shoulder. She nodded and smiled so I continued. "You have a lovely home," I said, mainly to be polite. Now I knew why the house looked worn and unkept, obviously Mr. Wilson couldn't keep up repairs and maintenance and it was obvious Walter was either too lazy or too busy stealing, to help the poor old man out. At the very least he could have slapped some fresh paint on it.

"Thanks," he said in a shaky voice. "It's been in my family for generations. It's seen better days, just can't get the old body to do what I want it to," When he smiled at that only one side of his fragile, cracked lips moved. Stroke perhaps? "Never had any trouble like this here before. But Steve here says I have ghosts."

"Possibly, Mr. Wilson, possibly," Steve stressed, but still with a sparkle in his voice. How does he do that? I could've said the same exact thing and it would have sounded sarcastic.

The old man turned shakily to face the house. Fearing he was about to fall, all of us lunged forward in unison. He continued, not noticing our brave attempt to save him. "I remember when my grandpappy built this house. Nothin' but farmland as far as the eye could see." Now, why did that sound familiar? He made a wide gesture with his arm and this time he did almost fall. We were at the ready. He caught himself and continued. "Grandpappy was one of the original settlers of Springfield." Really, I thought to myself. It was written everywhere that the Avery's were the original settlers of Springfield.

"How old were you when the house was built?" I asked, now curious. Got that from my mom and her love of houses. The home was rundown, but the structure was still intact. Also, if his granddad built the house, he wouldn't have been born.

"Oh pert 'near, three," he hesitated for a second to think, "No four years of age. He finished it right before my fourth birthday. But this weren't my grandpappy's first house." He swerved to his left and yet again almost fell over and yet again, we lunged. Okay, that's it! I'm buying him a cane! The old man had spunk, but his body, not so much. "The original sat right there were Nancy lives." He looked back at us and wiggled his eyebrows and half smiled, "she's a cutie that one." We all grinned at this bit of juicy information.

"How long have Walter and Brynn rented from you?" I said, steering the conversation back on track before that subject started to get too graphic.

"Goin' on about six months now," he said, facing us again. "Nice kiddos those two, paid their rent on time, took care of the inside perty well. Hard to believe they were doing anything bad." Nice, I thought. One was a thief and the other an accessory to a crime. Poor, sweet old guy was clueless who he had renting from him.

"Sometimes nice people get in with the wrong people," Riley said sympathetically. I glanced over at her. It wasn't what she said, but how she said it. Like she knew something else had happened that caused Walter to steal the painting. She looked over at me and shrugged. Okay, I will be delving into that later.

"Very true, Riles," Steve said, apparently not picking up on what I had. He turned to the elderly man, "Well Mr. Wilson, we will get set up and see if anything is amiss. Thank you for letting us into your home. We will let you know what we find."

The old man nodded and pulled out a ring with keys on it. At first, I thought he would be leaving the house keys with Steve, but he stumbled down the stairs and headed for an old turquoise Mercury Comet. The poor car looked pathetic, but fixed up, could be a gold mine. Then it hit me…was he about to drive? Note to self: if you see a turquoise Comet on the road, make an immediate U-ey and head the other way.

As we began pulling equipment from the van to set up inside the house, the weather took a nasty turn. When we were talking with Mr. Wilson, there were clouds but not these nasty black and gray clouds hanging over us now. While this kind of weather makes for great ghost hunting, on the Texas coast, it could get super bad…super-fast! I checked the local weather app on my phone. No special warnings popped up, so for now we were good.

Steve sent Riley and I into the garage to set up infrared cameras since this is where we first saw the spirit of the little girl. Steve didn't have any of these types of cameras the last time we hunted with him. Riley, ever curious, asked what they did. He explained that it detects and measures the thermal energy of objects or people. While I looked completely lost at this explanation, Riley didn't. A smile and a long drawn-out cool was her response. I shook my head and guided her towards the garage. I would make sure she explained it to me later.

Walter's car still sat in the same spot, so I decided to place one of the cameras facing the driver and passenger seats and one facing the back of the car which in that position would also catch any activity from the door leading to the interior of the house.

"How does this look?" I said into the mouthpiece. We were all assigned headsets so we could keep tabs on one another during the investigation. In previous investigations we used walkies to communicate which was more difficult to use especially when you had a Digital Audio Recorder in one hand and a Mel Meter in another. Using headsets left the hands free.

Colton was a tech genius and made a lot of the equipment used for the investigations. He asked me to move the camera angle so that the door leading into the house was more visible. I obeyed, moving it a smidge to the left. I was given a 10-4 over the headset. With our cameras in place, we headed back to the van where everyone was waiting. Guess Riley and I were a little rusty. We were the last to arrive and we only had two cameras.

"Okay, that looks to be everyone," Steve said, "Because the house isn't that big, we will alternate in groups of two. Stephi and Riley, I want you two to go in first to see if you can get the spirit to show herself." Most spirits were reluctant to appear, but since the little girl had already been in contact with Riley, sending us in first made the most sense. Colton handed me a Digital Audio Recorder (DAR), a device that recorded sounds like a recorder. When played back, if there were any voices or sounds it would capture it and we could hear it. We were also given little flashlights in case we needed them.

I looked at Riley, "Ready to do this?" She glanced at Celeste who smiled and nodded her support.

71

"Ready, Freddy. Let's do this!"

That's my girl! We headed slow and steady through the front door. After the ghost in the car incident, caution was key. The living room immediately felt heavy, not light and airy like the last time I was here. It was pitch dark, so Riley and I walked shoulder to shoulder until our eyes adjusted.

"You feel anything?" I asked with a whisper.

"No, but it feels heavy in here, do you feel it?"

"Yeah, felt it when we walked in. Let's see if we can get something on the DAR." I switched on the flashlight so I could make out which button to push for record. "Riley and Stephi DAR session in the living room." Steve had all investigators say who they were and what part of the building they were in. This helped the crew when going back over the recording cross reference any video with the recording. "Riles, you start. She will probably be more likely to answer you."

"Um, Hi." I could tell by the tone in her voice she was nervous. I felt her relax when I placed my hand on her shoulder for reassurance. "Hi, Elizabeth. My name is Riley and this is my mom, Stephi. We are here to help. Can you tell us what you need?"

"Why are you here in this house?" I asked pausing in case we got a response, then continued. "Is it because the painting is here?" Another pause. "Can you tell us how you died?" I stopped the recorder and turned on my mini flashlight so I could see the button for rewind. "Okay baby girl, let's see if we got anything."

I hit rewind and the recorder purred to life until it couldn't go back any further. I hit the play button and we both moved our heads closer to the machine. When it got to Riley's question there was

72

nothing. My first question yielded no answer, then at the second question, we heard a faint voice, but couldn't make out what was said. We continued on, not pausing to listen to it again. Because it was so faint, we would need to use headphones. Okay, only one question remained…the name. The voice returned, but not in a whisper. This one was clear! 'Lisbeth'.

"Did you hear that!" we both said simultaneously.

Steve came on the headset. "Okay girls, come on back out. I want to listen to those recordings."

As we started toward the door, we heard a loud bang. Riley and I turned quickly and grabbed each other's arms. "Steve, did y'all hear that?" I said into the mouthpiece as Riley and I slowly started toward the area where we thought the sound came from. Our flashlights were off so our eyes had to adjust again. "We're checking it out." A 'copy that' and 'be careful' came through the headset. Steve knew how green we still were at investigating.

Suddenly Riley just stopped. "Riles, you okay?"

"Yeah, give me a sec." We stood there. Her fingernails started to dig into my skin, but I said nothing and waited. "The attic. It's in the attic," she said finally.

"Steve, where in the house is the attic?" He relayed the owner mentioned in the walk-through that the attic was in the hallway leading to the bedrooms.

I switched on my flashlight as Riley and I stood under the attic door. A small rope dangled from the wood. I knew from experience that you had to literally yank on these strings. Reaching up I yanked. Nothing. It didn't budge. Okay, I know I'm not that weak. I handed my gear to Riley, time to put my weight to good use. With both hands, I yanked hard. The door let out a moan but only slightly moved. What the friggin' hell! Why was it so hard to open? I've opened our attic door at home a gazillion times! I let go briefly to rub my hands together and then on my jeans. I was gonna get that door open just out sheer tenacity. Gripping the rope and clearing my mind I pulled with my entire weight, my feet literally leaving the floor. The door swung down so hard and easily that I almost ran into it. It was like someone had been keeping me from getting it open. But no one was in the attic, actually no one was in the house period, except Riley and I. And surely the ghost wouldn't keep us from going in, the girl was the one, obviously, showing us where to find it. Or would she? Only one way to find out.

The door was inching its way closed so I pulled them down again, slowly this time, and started to head up. Adrenaline was pouring through my veins and all I wanted was to find that painting and the noise. I felt Riley's hand on my arm and I glanced down. "Mom, take the flashlight. And please, be careful."

"I will, promise." I flipped on the light and as I ascended, "Steve, I'm headed into the attic." A 10-4, which meant 'message received' in radio jargon. The steps were just wide enough to put the tip of my shoe on it, so I didn't have a choice but to go slowly. Once inside the attic, a familiar smell wafted toward me. The wonderful aroma was light and sweet like vanilla. I felt myself being drawn to it. As I involuntarily moved toward the smell, my mind searched, trying to place the origin of the smell. And then it hit me! Coffee? French Vanilla to be exact. I stopped dead. Another rope, well this was more like a string, lightly bopped against my forehead. I grabbed the string and pulled. Instantly the entire attic was flooded with light. My eyes quickly adjusted and I continued toward the coffee smell which now made sense as to why I was enchanted by its aroma. It was my favorite coffee.

On the east side of the attic, I found the source of the coffee. A Keurig machine sat on a huge chest nestled against the wall. Obviously, someone has been staying here. A homeless person? The house has been vacant since Walter and Brynn had gone MIA but not long enough for someone to take up residence. "Steve, I think you need to come up here," I said into the mouthpiece.

I continued to explore while waiting for Steve. Riley had already joined me. "Do you feel anything?" I asked her, hoping she could sense the ghost and lead us to the painting. She shook her head no and continued to search the west side of the attic. I stayed on the east side. Someone definitely had been living here because there were pillow and blankets nestled against the wall. An old radio sat next to the coffee machine and what I assume was a pile of dirty clothes sat in an old rocking chair.

Riley and I had been searching in silence when a deafening scream ripped through the quiet like fingernails on a chalkboard. My first thought was Riley and her safety. I literally ran to her thinking she had been hurt, but the scream wasn't from her, it was from…. Brynn?

Chapter Ten

Before I could ask anything, Steve appeared. Seeing Brynn standing there, and before I could explain he demanded. "Who the hell are you?"

"This is Brynn." I said moving to stand next to her. "She and her fiancé Walter are the ones renting the house." I turned back to face her. "Have you been up here all this time? Why did you call me and disappear?"

The look on her face was pure fear. Something had frightened her to the point of holding up in the attic. But if it was something in the house, why did she stay here. A million questions raced through my brain and I wanted answers, now!

"I-I'm, um. It wasn't me."

"Yes, it *was* you, Brynn. You said it was you and I recognized your voice." I turned to Steve. "I think we need to call the police."

"No!" she said emphatically. "You can't call the cops, please Stephi."

"Brynn you have been holed up in the attic. And you called me pleading with me to come help you, why?"

She stood there, rolling her hands together, hesitant to say anything but knowing she would have too. Either to me or the cops. "You won't believe me."

"You'd be surprised, trust me. Now spill it." I was angry, but also sympathetic. I just wanted answers.

"I was sitting in the car, my cell phone in my hand, ready to call you.… then." She hesitated, trying to find the courage to just say it.

"I saw a ghost!" she blurted out. She slumped, relieved as if a huge load had been taken off her shoulders. There was silence.

Finally, Riley spoke up. "A little girl, right?"

Brynn looked at her, surprised. "Yes! How did you know?" she continued before Riley could answer. "It freaked me out. I dropped my phone while getting out of that car. I've been up here ever since, wondering if I was crazy. Did I really see a ghost?"

"You're not crazy." Riley said in a comforting tone. "I've seen her too. Actually, more than seen, but that's another story."

"Okay, so who called me?" I chimed in.

Riley looked at me as if to say, 'you know who'. Which I suspected but didn't want to believe that a ghost could dial a phone number. I mean wouldn't her finger just go right through the phone. I knew they could touch objects or at least their energy could, but to physically dial a number. Well, I guess I would just have to chalk this up as another learning experience about the paranormal.

"That might explain the phone call, but not why you're hold up in the attic. What's the story there?" Brynn began to explain that after she saw the ghost she bolted out of the side door of the garage. She was headed for a friends house when the sky opened up and it began to pour...again. There was no choice but to go back to their house.

"I figured I would be okay in the house since the garage is where I had seen the ghost. I was wrong. The little girl was everywhere! I tried to leave again, but she wouldn't let me out. I pulled on unlocked doors only to find they wouldn't budge. So, I grabbed some food and went to the attic. I figured if I couldn't leave, at least I could have my own space. Funny, she never came up here. Guess she gave me my space."

"Why wouldn't she let you leave?" Riley asked, mainly to herself. She was curious of the actions of the little girl, I knew. Brynn shook her head and shrugged thinking Riley was asking her the question.

"Well, you're okay now," I interceded putting an arm around Brynn.

"We need to do a spirit box session," Steve said. "We have to find out what she wants." Only once during an investigation had I seen the Spirit box used so it was still somewhat new to me. Well, all of this was new to me. If memory served, two people were used to conduct the session. One would ask questions while the other would put on a blindfold and headphones so they could hear any voices. The spirit box was basically a box that had white noise and when a question was asked the person wearing the blindfold and headphones would listen for any key words pertaining to the question and blurt them out.

We all agreed, except Brynn, she was still freaked out about all the ghost stuff happening. I suggested she stay at a hotel for the night when Steve pulled me to the side out of earshot of the others.

"She might be of some help to us," he suggested. I wasn't sure how, but Steve knew more than I did about this, so I nodded for him to continue. "I know she is freaked out by all of this, but she did survive up here for a few days..."

"And?" I knew more was coming.

"And, if she survived up here, without incident, with the painting supposedly up here with her then the ghost is used to her and between Riley and Brynn we might get more answers."

This theory did make sense. We still needed to find out why the ghost wouldn't let Brynn leave and it's possible the ghost tried to communicate with her where the painting was located but Brynn was too freaked out to realize this. It wasn't going to be an easy task convincing her. Like she was super freaked out! Shaking and ranting incoherently was her M.O. at the moment. "We can give it a shot," was my response, and I regretted it as soon as I said it because I knew what was coming, so I added, "but there are no guarantees."

Naturally, Steve chose me for this particular task, some blather about my connection with Brynn and she trusted me. Whatever, I was not very happy about it. I took a couple of deep breaths, gave Steve a look that said, 'back me up if I need it or I'll kick your ass!', and I moved toward Brynn who now sat on the rocking chair, the pile of clothes that previously resided there had been thrown to the ground.

I cleared my throat. "Brynn," she looked up at me with frightened eyes. She was still shaking but not as much and the hysterical ranting was gone. "Steve thinks…," I glanced over at Steve who gave me a thumbs up so I continued, "Steve and I think that it would be a good idea," no that wasn't a good start, I thought, "We think the ghost likes you and wants you to help her. If you stayed with us for the night and tried to communicate with her, we can find out why she's here and how to help her." I was taking a chance pulling on Brynn's heartstrings when the girl was clearly a train wreck, but that might be what would pull her into helping us.

There was a long silence. Too long for me. I blew it. I probably scared her even more with the suggestion of staying here. Earlier when I had said it would be a good idea for her to leave she looked slightly relieved, but now she was slumped over, her head in hands that rested on her knees. Suddenly she lifted her head and slapped her knees with the palms of her hands and said, "I'm tired of being scared, if you need my help. I'll do it!"

We all jumped at this sudden revelation. "Um, okay cool," was all I managed to get out. Steve, on the other hand, had a different reaction.

"That's great!" Steve said clapping his hands together as he moved toward us, "I've been thinking maybe have Brynn sit in on the Spirit Box session. Specifically asking the questions." He hesitated for a second to see Brynn's reaction. She nodded a yes and he continued, "Awesome! Riley will have the headphones on listening for any communication from the little girl."

I was happy Steve was happy, but I still had a sinking feeling Brynn might freak out again. Yes, she did agree to the spirit box. However, she has never sat in on one of these before, heck I have only done this once so I was still a little skeptical. But I would give her the benefit of the doubt...for now.

We all agreed the best place to do the session was right where we were...the attic. Which made sense. Riley said she felt the painting was in the house, but not specifically where in the house so since we were already here, might as well start here. And this way we could start from the top and finish in the main house. Steve had brought his video camera, which was permanently attached to his hand in my opinion, when he initially came up here so he could film the spirit box session.

Steve explained how the session would work as Riley positioned herself on the opposite side of the attic from them per his instruction. Something about less interference was all I got. I chose to stand close to her. My nerves were on edge. A wave of emotions flooded over my body. This was her first session since discovering her gift and I wasn't sure if she could handle it. Which was stupid of course, I knew how strong she was. I pulled one side of the headphones from her ear and whispered, "You got this. Love you bunches." She gave me a weak smile and nodded.

Steve gave us the silent signal which meant we were starting. Riley turned on the spirit box. We heard nothing, but she could hear the white noise through the headphones. On the other side, I heard Brynn clear hear throat.

"W-what is your n-name?" she asked, you could hear the trembling in her voice, but there was also determination in it as well. Riley said nothing so Brynn continued with the list of questions given to her.

"Is your name Elizabeth?"

"Yes."

"Are you here with us now?

"Yes," Riley blurted out. "Help."

"Stop."

"Can't."

"No."

Steve told Brynn to continue. "It's okay. Riley is saying everything that comes through clearly. Go ahead."

"Elizabeth where is the painting?"

"Car."

"Walter."

Was she telling us the painting was in Walter's car? Which wasn't good. The police had searched the Walter's car and yielded nothing.

"Why are you here? Why haven't you moved on?"

"Can't."

"Hurt."

"Kill."

That last one took us all by surprise. Steve and I locked eyes. We knew exactly what had happened to Elizabeth. She was murdered. But by who and why?

"Were you killed?" Brynn asked going off book. She was genuinely getting interested now.

"Yes."

"By whom?"

We waited for a few minutes with no response. Riley pulled the headphones off.

"There's nothing, she's gone. Well, she's not gone, gone. Just gone from this room." Riley said with sadness in her voice. I put my arm around her and gave her a hug.

"It's okay baby girl."

"She's sad mom. She wants to move on but can't. We've got to help her." Determination in her voice took the place of sadness. I knew that voice and when Riley set her mind to something, she was going to do it.

"She can count on us, for sure."

We investigated through the night, but it was quiet. No thumps, no voices, no possessions. Just silence. At five a.m. Steve called a wrap on the investigation. The crew had a lot of video and audio footage to go through which would take them a few days. Riley asked if she could help them, and I agreed. I told her I thought it would be good for her. I knew she would be in good hands with Steve and Celeste.

I slept through the next morning until after noon. It was Sunday and normally I gave Nana a break and cooked breakfast. I got up and washed my face to get the boogies out of my eyes and headed downstairs to the kitchen. Naturally coffee was the first thing I would make but as I got closer I could smell the sweet aroma of caramel macchiato wafting toward me.

"Ah, there you are!" Nana said sprinkling seasoning on the hash browns in the skillet after which she added eggs, onion, and sausage it would become a breakfast skillet. Now these were not store-bought hash browns, but homemade and the best in the county. I told her that she needed to keep a recipe book so when she croaked I could cook as good as her. She would laugh because she knew once she was gone, Riley and I would be eating out.

"Morning. Smells yummy." I said, giving her a kiss on the cheek. She waved me off with her spatula as if she didn't like all that mushy stuff, but I knew there was a smile on her face as I sat down in front of the coffee she had already made for me. She might be a pain in the butt sometimes, but she was the best and I loved her.

"So, tell me all about last night." I could hear the curiosity in her voice.

I filled her in on the events of last night. How we found Brynn and the spirit box session. And finally, the highlight of the night, that the little girl Elizabeth had been killed. She stopped dead and turned to look at me. The surprise on her face was priceless!

"Are you shittin' me?" The police voice came out and I knew I had her full attention. She might not like ghost hunting, but police hunting was her specialty and she loved it.

I shook my head no and chuckled. "You should have seen the shock on all our faces when we heard it."

"I can imagine. Especially if you weren't expecting it." She turned off the burner, leaving the potatoes in the skillet, grabbed her coffee, and came to sit at the table with me. "So now we have a murder to solve on top of a theft."

"Yep," I took a sip of coffee, "and we have nowhere to start." I knew this part would reel her in and she would be hooked. I could see the cop part of her brain starting to emerge and blam! There you have it people.

"Well, if you're ghosty buddies had access to information about the little girl, then they can dig even deeper and find out how she died. We can search online for any deaths relating to any girl her age with the name Elizabeth and see what we get. We know she is part of the Avery family, but they might have opted not to publish an obit for whatever reason." She hesitated like she was in a trance.

"What is it?"

"Well, they could cover it up by not publishing an obit but they would have to have buried her, gotten a death certificate, etc. We are going to have to dig super deep into this family's history."

"We could broaden our search to nearby counties or even a national search. Maybe they buried her outside of Springfield or Texas." I suggested, my mind starting to work like my mom's and when that happened we were unstoppable. "Hell, she could have been adopted for all we know."

Chapter Eleven

Riley spent all day Sunday with Steve going over footage. I was anxious to hear if they found anything. I knew it took a while, sometimes days, to go over all the footage from all the cameras which ran the entire night, but Steve had a lot of people so maybe it would take as long. It was close to seven o'clock p.m. and I couldn't stand waiting. I'm not known for my patience, so my text with her went something like this...

Me: Hey baby girl. Did y'all find anything?

Riley: Hey mom. Not yet. There is so much to look through.

Riley: Celeste had to leave early and one of the other guys, think he's new, isn't very efficient. Those are Steve's words, not mine. Lol

Me: Yeah, I know it takes time. When will you be home?

Riley: Steve said we should be done by tomorrow morning maybe late afternoon.

Me: You have school tomorrow.

Riley: Come on Mom! Please let me stay! I can afford to miss one more day.

I thought about it for a minute or so before responding. She was a straight-A student, it was a Monday so she wouldn't have any tests, and she had only missed one other day.

Me: Okay but keep me posted on what's going on. Love you!

Riley: Thanks, Mom! Love you bunches!

And that's the softy I am. I went in search for Nana to update her on, well, nothing really, and found her in the kitchen on her laptop. Mine sat across from her open and ready, for researching was my guess. She was so engrossed in what she was doing she didn't notice me come in. I made a cup of coffee, thinking that would get her attention and she would ask for one as well. Nothing.

"Penny for your thoughts," I said making my presence known. Still, nothing. "Okay Ma, what has you so engrossed that you're ignoring me?" I said and set my coffee on the table before sitting in front of my laptop.

I guess it was the tone I used because she glanced up at me. "You need to call Brynn to see when we can stop by. There are some questions we need to ask her."

"What questions? Did you find something out?" I sat up in my chair, curiosity had engulfed every fiber of my body. But it would soon be doused at her next words.

"Make the appointment and you'll see," was all she said.

Are you serious! That was all she was going to tell me! Which is exactly what I said to her. Why was she keeping information from me. If I knew my mom, and I knew her all too well, she was about to expose something.

"I'm not sure of all the details yet, but by the time we go see Brynn I will have what I need." She went back to her laptop which told me the conversation was over and if I tried to pry the information out of her, she would ream my butt up one side and down the other. And that was something I strived to avoid with her. It was still early so I called Brynn and asked if we could stop by tomorrow. She said two o'clock would be good for her and I agreed. We said our goodbyes and I relayed the information to Nana.

We worked silently until about eleven p.m. when suddenly after checking her phone Nana stretched and yawned. "Time for bed. We'll discuss more tomorrow." She closed her laptop and headed to her room which was on the first floor. Mine and Riley's rooms were upstairs. I sat back and stared after her until I heard her door close. What the hell was going on. While I was used to her acting this way when she was still on the force, since her retirement we were both open books, told each other everything. Well, almost everything. There were still some things I kept from her but nothing serious or especially information pertaining to a case. Well, I didn't have a choice but to wait, so I closed my laptop and headed upstairs the whole time grumbling "I better get answers tomorrow or else! Friggin' not tell me anything. Really?!"

The next morning it was like nothing had happened the night before. She was at the stove cooking breakfast as usual as I sauntered into the kitchen heading straight to the coffee machine.

"Finally! I guess I need to buy you a second alarm clock for when Riley isn't here to wake you up." Well, I'm glad her ability to fuss at me hadn't changed!

"I kept researching after going upstairs, so I didn't get to sleep until around one a.m."

"Find anything?" she asked putting a yummy plate of eggs, toast and sausage in front of me.

"Well, I checked the surrounding counties for any deaths of a child that was six years old with the name Elizabeth."

"And...."

"A lot! So many I closed my laptop and decided to pick it back up today."

"Like how many?" She said sitting across from me with her own yummy plate. "That's kind of unusual to have 'a lot' of six-year-olds named Elizabeth having died."

"Well, Texas' vital statistics has records dating back to the early 1900's, so yeah there were 'a lot'. But you're right, that was an excessive amount, so I googled pandemics in the 1900's." I took a bite and continued, "from 1918 to 1920 the Spanish Flu pandemic took about half a million lives in Americans. I couldn't find how many in Texas, but I did find that the oil fields in Texas were hit hard by the flu because of poor working conditions and lack of health care." I paused to take another bite.

"My goodness, you did do your research," Nana said with a smile. She knew history wasn't one of my best subjects in school so me spouting out statistics from the 1900's was very unusual.

"Sorry, guess old age makes me want to learn more." We both laughed at that. I wasn't that old but man if it wasn't creeping up on me, ready to pounce.

"Don't apologize. It's some good information, actually. What if the little girl was a victim of the Spanish flu?" Nana took a sip of coffee before continuing. "I mean she was wearing a poofy pink dress with a bow in her hair, right?"

"Um, I remember you dressing me up in pink frilly dresses," I said smiling. I was an only child, so I was pretty spoiled but if I messed up, I paid the price. Which would depend on the crime. Not an actual crime, oh hell no, I wouldn't be here right now if I had committed any real crimes. Nana loved me and spoiled me but step a toe out of line in our household growing up and there would be hell to pay. Dang, my mind wandered yet again!

"Yes, I did, and I would do it again."

"Okay back to Elizabeth. She could have been born and died anytime, doesn't have to be in the early 1900's, could have been in the early 2000's. That's what I need to find out as soon as we get to the office."

We cleaned our breakfast plates and headed out. We took Nana's car because we were picking Riley up on the way to see Brynn later and Riley doesn't like my music so....

On the way, Riley text me. When I'm driving I have it on driving mode so when Riley sees that, she knows to text Nana. "What did she say," I ask after hearing the beep for the message received on her phone.

"She said she should be done around noon. Steve said he and the new guy could handle what was left."

"Great! Did she say they found anything?"

"Nope, that was it."

"Okay," there was clearly disappointment in my voice.

We arrived at the office around nine. Nana went to turn on the lights and I went straight for the coffee machine. I was hoping she would bring up what happened last night but as she walked from the back room it was clear that was not going to come to pass. She went straight for her computer as did I when my coffee was done. Whatever. This was ridiculous, there was no reason whatsoever for her to keep vital information from me. And I was about to lay into her when the phone rang. Ugh!

"Lane Private Detective Agency," I snapped, "whaddya want!" I cringed and looked at Nana. She raised an eyebrow that said, 'excuse me?' I wanted to take the words back as soon as I said them but of course, I couldn't. It wasn't my fault I was a Ghostbusters movie fanatic. And besides if it hadn't been for Nana irritating me before work, I wouldn't have been so testy. It made me feel a bit better blaming my attitude on her, but I knew it was all my fault for letting it bother me. I managed to mutter out, "Um how can I help you?"

"Ms. Cay, it's Argus Pittman from State Insurance," he said still taken aback by my bad behavior.

"I am so sorry, Mr. Pittman, bad morning," was my lame excuse for acting unprofessional.

He laughed, "No worries Ms. Cay, we all have bad mornings."

Yeah, that might be true, but I was always mindful of my professionalism with clients. "What can I do for you Mr. Pittman?" I said bouncing back easily.

"We are calling to perhaps get an update on the case." There he went again with the 'we' thing. However, this time I think I know who the 'we' consisted of. Mr. Avery. It had to be because he had already made an appearance at our office. Unannounced I might add. I updated him on what we had so far and concluded with we were close to finding the painting. Which was not at all true. Well, it was partially true. We knew it had to be in the house somewhere, which is why I suggested to Nana that we get with Steve on a possible return to the Mayhew house after filling her in on my conversation with Mr. Pittman. She agreed and told me to set it up. Yes, she actually agreed with me on another ghost hunt.

We worked in silence until it was time to get Riley. I flipped the "will be back soon' sign on the door, locked up and we headed to pick up Riley. The ride to Steve's ghost-hunting office didn't take long, but the silence in the car made it seem like it took forever. Steve's office was a small brick building that sat in between two large buildings. We parked in the back of the building for lack of no parking in the front. Inside we found Riley sitting in front of a computer monitor. When she saw us she clicked pause, pulled off the headphones and waved us over. She must be listening for any sounds or voices and looking for anything out of the ordinary from the investigation. I remembered having that job when I helped Steve on cases.

"Hey baby girl, you about done?" I asked kissing her on the head.

"Hey mom, Nana. Yeah, I've got about ten more minutes of footage to go through and then we can go." I could tell she was tired and hadn't slept much, if at all.

"Sounds good. I have to talk to Steve anyway. Know where I can find him?"

She slipped the headphones back on and pointed to a small office across from where she sat. The walls and door were all glass and I could see Steve on the phone at his desk. I knocked on the door and he waved me in. In front of his desk sat two old leather chairs that looked like they belonged in the 1950's. I checked some emails on my phone while I waited for him to finish his call. I couldn't help but overhear his side of the conversation which apparently was a potential client by the way he was taking notes on a pad and letting the person know that they would find out what was happening at their home and that when children were involved they always put the case ahead of everything else. Which meant that a trip back to the Mayhew house would probably not happen anytime soon. He hung up the phone, sat back and took a deep breath.

"Hey kiddo, what kind of trouble are stirring up?" Trouble? Me? I just laughed but in the back of my mind, I was thinking I wasn't the one about to stir up trouble but an old, retired police officer was, I knew it.

"Not much. Just came by to take Riley off your hands." I said making small talk before asking about going back into the Mayhew house. "She been driving you nuts?"

He smiled. "You know she doesn't drive me nuts. She's a very good investigator and has been a lifesaver going over all the footage from the Mayhew house."

"Give her time, she'll try to start bossing you around," I paused, then added, "politely, of course."

"I'll make a mental note of that one. So, did you have a question for me, or did you come to visit me because of my good looks?'

I rolled my eyes and smiled. Steve wasn't bad-looking by a long shot. However, he wasn't a 'faint when you see him guy either. He towered over me at 6'1, had dark brown hair, and his eyes were bluer than mine, if that was possible. And I could be mistaken but I had a feeling he had a soft spot for me. I giggled, oh my gosh just like my mom…ick! "Let's say both."

He laughed. "Okay, I can take a hint when it's time to change the subject. What's your question?"

"Well," I began, hesitantly because I knew how busy he was. "Nana and I thought it would be good idea to go back to the Mayhew house. Or if your too busy, we could go in by ourselves."

"Two things you need to know, Stephi. One I am never too busy for you." He looked at the calendar in front of him. It was one of those that sat on the desk where you could quickly glance at it. "And two, my crew is experienced enough that they can handle any case without me." He smiled at me that made me uncomfortable and comfortable at the same time. Weird. "When did you have in mind?"

"We are on our way to talk to Brynn after we leave here, so I will see when is convenient for her."

"Good deal. Just give me a call when you know."

Right then Riley walked in and announced she was finally finished. Steve and I both stood up. "Thanks for taking the time to help Steve, I really appreciate it."

"Anytime. I look forward to hearing from you." With that said Riley gave me a 'what's that suppose to mean' look. I ignored it and we left, quickly.

We all piled into the car and as soon as the car doors shut Riley pounced on me like a lioness and her prospective kill.

"Omg, mom!" The tone in her voice told me she wanted answers. "Do you and Steve have a thing going?"

"Don't be ridiculous Riley." My tone on the other hand was completely defensive and she sensed it, even if I was denying, denying, denying. "Steve and I have been friends since high school. He's like a brother to me." I glanced at her in the rearview mirror. Nope, she wasn't buying it. Okay, then we change the subject. "So,

Nana what is the plan for Brynn?" A huge sigh came from the back of the car. Riley was not happy with me right now. Oh well, she'd just have to get over it.

She looked shocked as if I'd caught her off guard, but I knew differently, she was feigning dumb. Rolling my eyes, I started the car, knowing she wasn't going to budge. I don't even know why I tried. Oh wait. Because I was getting out of the conversation about Steve. Riley and Nana chatted while I drove and ran scenarios through my head on what was about to go down. The obvious was she knew something I didn't. But what? Did she know where Walter Mayhew was? Did she know where the painting was? Ugh! the painting. It was the center of this entire investigation, and we still were nowhere near finding it. We had searched the house from top to bottom and still nothing. Before I could search my brain any further, we had reached the Mayhew house. I pulled into the driveway and put the car in park. "Here we are," I said as we all climbed out of the car.

I knocked on the front door. The silence between us as we waited for Brynn was deafening. The door opened so fast that all three of us jumped simultaneously. Seriously. I was expecting a demure, reserved Brynn instead we were greeted with a jovial, energetic version of her. All that went through my brain at that moment was "Huh?"

"I am so glad to see all of you," she said ushering us into the house. Because we were still in shock we did as we were told. We all sat on the sectional couch while Brynn sat across from us in an oversized chair that looked like it was from the turn of the century. "So, what did you want to talk about?"

"Well," I began, but I was quickly cut off.

"We have some unfortunate news to tell you," Nana said trying to sound sympathetic, but sucking at it. Brynn's jovial appearance quickly changed to the demure I was expecting earlier. "Walter is dead."

I swear I felt my jaw drop as my head swung toward my mother. The look on her face was not sympathetic, but accusatory. I could probably ask, but I knew my mom, she was about to drop the H-bomb on Brynn. So, this was the big secret. This is what she couldn't tell me? Oh, hell no, we will be going to fist city over this one later.

"I am so sorry we had to deliver this news to you," I said quickly, cutting my eyes toward Nana. I had to try and cover my surprise at this information as Brynn was probably thinking I already knew of Walter's death. However, it was I that was surprised once more with Brynn's reaction. Normally someone who found out their fiancé was dead would be bawling like someone had turned on a water faucet. But not her, she laid her hands in her lap and…wait, was she trying to drum up some tears? Her body was stiff and after a few minutes, she actually did manage to get a few tears out. After all that energy getting the tears, she grabbed a tissue from the box on the coffee table and dabbed each eye. Well, I felt stupid! I had felt sorry for this girl when we first got here, but now I knew something was up with her.

I heard a deep sigh next to me and knew Nana had had enough of the act she was putting on. "Yes, we are sorry to have to bring this unfortunate news but let's be real here Brynn."

She looked at Nana with what could have been a clueless expression but let's be honest, she wasn't that good of an actress. "Excuse me?" Brynn said still trying to look oblivious.

"I know you were involved in Walter's death." Now this was worse than the H-bomb from earlier and I was getting angrier by the minute, but I held my composure for the time being.

"Are you mad!" Brynn shot back. "Walter and I were getting married. Why would I kill my fiancé?" And that was all my mom needed.

"I didn't say you killed anyone," Nana was very calm and collected, a sign of a good policeman. "I said you were involved."

"I-I didn't…" this time the tears flowing were real and she was visibly shaking, and I knew I was finally about to find out the story when there was a knock on the door. Of course, there would be, why not? Riley and Nana didn't move and Brynn being in the state she was in, I guess I would be the one to get the door. I opened the door and the look of shock on my face must have been apparent because standing before me was Dougie who smiled politely, which I knew was a sign he was here on business. He entered and following behind was his 'new' partner which Nana had yet to meet, and I actually felt a smile form on my face. Ha! This time she would be the one shocked. I chuckled to myself as I closed the door.

Dougie wasted no time, "Miss Lewis, I have some questions to ask you about your fiancé Walter Mayhew." At this point Brynn was in full hysterics.

"I won't say anything in front of them!" She managed to get out through her rampage of hysteria.

Dougie nodded, "I'm sorry ladies," he directed at us, "but you will need to leave." Then to Nana, he said, "I will be in touch." We knew that we couldn't sit in on the questioning. As we were leaving I noticed Nana gave Dougie's new partner a dirty look which made me laugh. That's what you get for not sharing important information with me.

By the time we left it was late and we were hungry. I didn't think picking a fight in car was a good decision, so I decided to wait until we got back to the office. But first, we would get food and I would get the full story. We all agreed on our favorite haunt, Burger Joint. While I wasn't looking forward to seeing Sam drool all over my mom, I was really looking forward to a burger, and this time there would be no theft of hamburgers by Nana.

When we got there Sam did his usual routine of swooning over Nana, we order and sat at one of the tables. I made my mom order a burger this time and a salad just in case she changed her mind. Sam delivered our food, drooled over Nana some more before running off to help more customers. After we had devoured half of our food we sat back to take a break before digging into the second half. The great thing about Sam's place is you get more food for your buck. Sometimes more than you can eat in one sitting, but we were really hungry.

I started because I was the one out of the loop. I noticed at Brynn's house that Riley was as calm as Nana, so I sensed she knew something as well. It was obvious she was in on some if not all of Nana's plan.

"Okay, who wants to tell me what's going on?" I had strategically sat across from them so I could make eye contact with both at the same time. They looked at each other. Riley pointed at herself and Nana nodded. "Well? I'm waiting."

"It happened after we texted Sunday." I knew Riley was nervous because she was fiddling with her fries. "I was going through the DVR tape from the camera they had set up in the garage." She sat up straight before continuing, "I saw Walter in the car holding the painting."

"Like you saw him alive? Or you saw his ghost?" I asked stupidly because of course he was a ghost, but for some reason I needed clarification.

"He was a ghost. But…" she paused before continuing, "when I saw that, I closed my eyes and I could sense him, nothing strong. And then in my head I heard the word," she hesitated. Why was she hesitating? She knew I didn't like dramatic pauses.

"What Riley?!" I was getting mad and anxious.

"Matty," she said quietly.

Okay didn't see that one coming. "Matty, as in Matthew? As in possibly Matthew Avery?"

"We think so," Nana added.

"We? Are you talking about Dougie now?"

"Yes, okay! As soon as I heard the name, I contacted Dougie."

"What is wrong with the two of you? Why didn't either one of you let me know?" I was heated by this time and my voice rose a bit, so I put myself in check. Well, and the look on Nana's face told me I better lower my voice.

"Look, don't be mad at Riley. I told her to keep quiet because I wanted to get some intel on Matty's whereabouts." She paused before continuing. "I know you, Stephi, if you had known about this you would have gone straight over to Brynn's and blown the whole thing. Not on purpose, of course. And well, I wanted to shock the crap out of her into telling the truth."

True, I would have because I had been sympathetic toward Brynn and to find out she was involved in Walter's disappearance and possibly his death would have put me over the edge. But I wasn't done with the fight. "You told Riley," I said sounding like a child who was being kept out of the loop.

"Not everything." Wow, that made me feel so much better. Geez, there was that child again.

"Okay, so what did you find out about Matty? And how is he involved in this?" The story of Matty and his pregnant wife came to mind. Maybe we were looking for the wrong daughter and wrong male Avery. "Listen, and this could be farfetched, but I don't think so."

"What?" Riley and Nana said at the same time. Riley quickly said from the side of her mouth, "Jinx." There was that thing between the two of them again so I ignored it.

"What if the painting of the little girl is Matty's daughter and not Mr. Avery's sister? Remember when we went to the museum and what's her name, Angela, said the painting was of Mr. Avery's sister. What if they just told everyone that it was the elder Avery's daughter to cover Matty's mistake?" They sat quiet, anxiously waiting for my next words. It was kind of creepy. "I remember reading that Matty's ex-wife and his daughter were living in another state. What if something happened to the little girl?"

"Okay, but why would she be haunting the Mayhew house?" Riley asked breaking the creepy stare she had on me which broke Nana's stare too.

I started to speak, not really thinking that part through but Nana saved me, "Maybe Matty didn't want the painting hanging in the art

100

museum, so he had Walter steal it. But Brynn took him out of the picture."

"Oh," Riley interrupted. "And what if Brynn and Walter only pretended to be engaged. That was their cover story so people wouldn't question why they spent so much time together."

"Right," I said, and added, "and Brynn didn't want to share the money with Walter, that's why she ousted him."

They both nodded at that. Dang, did we just solve part of the case? We sat there in silence for a while, soaking in the information we had just put together. I picked up the other half of my burger and everyone followed suit. We finished our food in silence and headed back to the office.

Chapter Twelve

As soon as we walked through the door, the phone rang. I was the closest, so I grabbed it while Nana turned on the lights and Riley went straight for her computer. I looked at the caller ID, it was the Springfield Police Department. It was Dougie. "Hey, Dougie," I said as I plopped down into my desk chair.

"How did you know it was me?" Came the response.

"Caller ID Dougie. I have to know what goobers are calling us."

"Ha. Ha." He said and then silence. I knew he was trying to think of a good comeback but couldn't. Then apparently giving up he just said, "Oh yeah."

"Okay I win that one, what's up?" I was hoping he had gotten something substantial from Brynn.

"You might want to put me on speaker so everyone can hear what I have to say." I did as he requested then snapped my fingers at Nana and Riley. "It's Dougie," I told them. Both of them converged to my desk.

"We are all here Dougie, whenever you're ready," I said to the phone.

"So, we ended up bringing Miss Lewis into the station. She was," he paused, and we heard a deep sigh come from the phone before he continued, "being irrational and became belligerent." Yeah, what he wanted to say is she was a pain in the rear end. "It took her about an hour alone in an interrogation room before we could actually talk to her reasonably. She did confess she helped Walter take the painting, so we are holding her on a theft charge.

But she is steadfast that she didn't kill Walter and doesn't know who did."

"That's a lie, she has to know who did it, even if she didn't do the actual killing," I said accusingly.

"Well, if she does, she's not saying," Dougie said matter of fact.

"Did she at least tell you who hired her and Walter to steal the painting?" Nana asked.

"Not yet, but given how fast she ratted out Walter, I'm sure it will be soon. I'll call when we have more information."

"Thanks, Dougie. We really appreciate your help. Talk to you soon." I clicked the off button on the phone and sat back in my chair. Nana and Riley were still standing in front of my desk.

"What are you two thinking?" I asked, curious for their input on what we just heard.

"Well, we know Brynn and Walter's engagement was the cover for the theft. She sat at the entrance and knew pretty much everything that went on." Nana started, "and if she is being steadfast about the killing part then we need to find some clues to who did kill Walter."

"Right," I agreed. "And find the painting. I still think another investigation at the Mayhew house is a good idea. Riley, maybe you can pick up something from Walter and what happened to Elizabeth." I smiled, "time to use those powers you have baby girl."

I set up a time with the owner of the house and called Steve to confirm he was available for the coming weekend. It was late and we were exhausted, so we closed up shop and headed home. It had been a long day and if we were going to wrap this case up, then we needed rest.

***

I woke up in a foul mood, probably for lack of sleep. Exhaustion had left me falling asleep in my clothes, which I hated, plus I tossed and turned most of the night thinking of ways to solve the case. I knew I needed to research some more, especially with our theory that Matty might be the father of Elizabeth and not what we had been told which Elizabeth was Mr. Avery's sister. Hold on. What if Elizabeth was Matty's sister! My brain went crazy with this new theory, and I was so excited to get downstairs and share it that I almost forgot to put my shoes on. Focus, Stephi, focus I said over and over in my head. Yeah, I'll focus when I get some coffee.

Downstairs in the kitchen was the same as always, Nana cooking breakfast and Riley jamming to tunes on her phone. Thank goodness she had earbuds in. I kissed her on the head and went for the coffee. "Morning," I said to Nana groggily and gave her a side hug. Silence followed, which was unusual. I looked over at her and she seemed to be in a trance. "What's wrong?" She just continued gently stirring the eggs. "Ma!" I snapped loudly.

"Huh? What are you yelling for?" She snapped back. Louder than I had because Riley pulled out her earbuds and asked what was wrong.

"Because I said morning, I gave you a hug and you still didn't say anything," I said matter-of-factly, "What's on your mind? The case?"

"Oh sorry. Yeah, I've been thinking about what we have so far." She turned off the stove, put some toast and eggs on a plate and shoved it in front of Riley. I guess she thought Riley would eat the eggs with her fingers because she forgot to give her a fork. I grabbed one from the drawer and placed it on Riley's plate. Nana's behavior didn't worry me, she acted this way when I was growing up. Her and Dougie would be on a case and it all but consumed her until they closed the case. But somehow this seemed a bit different.

"So, what are you thinking?" I asked which brought her back to the present.

"Riley, didn't you say you saw a figure of Walter Mayhew holding the painting when you going through the footage? Well, we know the painting is at the house, where we don't know yet." She paused for a moment, so I stepped in.

"Remember how Steve has told us that ghosts can haunt objects?" They both nodded. "Well, the reason would be obvious. If the painting is with Walter, and we know the painting is at the house, then it has to be *buried* with him. Which means…"

Riley took over this time, "which means he's buried on the property somewhere!"

"Right! Nana, we need to get in touch with Dougie so he can get another warrant to search the grounds." She was already on the phone punching in his number.

While she called Dougie, I turned to Riley. "Okay baby girl, we still need to find out why Elizabeth is still here and what happened to her."

"Yeah, and how Matty is tied into all of this," she added.

"Right, so we need to do some researching. I'll hit the computers after I drop you off, and I'll call Steve to see if we can move the date up to today for the investigation." She nodded. I knew she would be up for it. She always was. "There must be something, somewhere, and someone must know something about this little girl Elizabeth. And we're gonna find out!"

On the way to the school, Nana filled us in on what Dougie said. He would get with the owner of the house to get permission to dig which would be faster than getting a warrant. Since there was no real evidence, only a ghost on video with the painting, that Walter was buried there, a warrant could take anywhere from two hours to two weeks. But, getting consent from the owner, it wouldn't take as long. And they needed to jump on this quickly. Nana had also told Dougie our suspicions that Matty was involved somehow which led Dougie to tell her that Matty was currently in town. Which was an interesting bit of information. Why was he here? And why now?

At the office, I flipped on the computer. Nana did her usual flipping the lights and checking voicemails. I started my search on Matthew Avery. Since it had been eons ago that I searched anything on this guy and the internet was more sophisticated now, maybe there was information on what this guy has been doing for the past ten or so years. Right away a link to a profile of his, there were several, popped up. Not surprisingly he had more than one, he had always been a tad full of himself, even in high school. I started at the top, clicked on it and it took me to the main page. I moved the cursor over the profile icon and clicked. It had posts dated today, and some pictures of himself and his buds at a ski resort. Shocker. I scrolled through some more posts which were just more of the first post. I looked through his pictures, there were none with his daughter or ex-wife. Not surprising. On his profile he had listed living in Europe, nothing specific which meant he didn't want anyone knowing his exact location. But I needed information on his daughter and ex-wife. I needed to know if they were still alive, or at least the ex. I didn't even know if Elizabeth was his daughter's name.

I left Matty's profile page and switched gears to search the Springfield newspaper online for anything on him. I clicked on the archive section. After sifting through several articles, I found the one from high school. I skimmed through it, my eyes probably looking like I was at a tennis match, looking specifically for…bam! There it was in black and white…Amanda Pierce. I hit the desk with such force that Nana looked over at me like, what the hell! "Sorry," I said quietly since she was on the phone.

My next search would take me to a profile page of Amanda Pierce. I read through her details; she lived in Washington State with her daughter…aww man! I hit the desk again, garnering another dirty look from Nana. Her daughter's name is Shelby. Well, that is that. I sat back in my chair deciding my next move. Then it hit me Shelby was her first name, but what was her middle name? I scrolled through more of Amanda's photos, posts, and friends list. I came across some older posts when Shelby was born. Amanda introduced her new daughter as Shelby Elizabeth Avery. Yes! I nearly peed my pants from excitement. Finally! And then I found it. One of Amanda's friends commented on how pretty the name was and she commented back that she just loved the name Shelby, and the name Elizabeth was in honor of Matty's deceased sister. Holy crap! Elizabeth was Matty's sister.

"Ma!" I shouted. I was so excited I didn't care if she was on the phone, I found the connection. I kept my eyes on the computer screen afraid that the information would disappear if I looked away. I could hear her politely apologize for my rudeness and that she would get back with them soon. I'm assuming it was a future client.

"Stephi that was extremely rude!" she chastised vehemently after hanging up the phone.

"I know, I'm sorry." I pointed to the screen, still staring at it. "Come look what I found."

"What?" she asked with a little bit too much sarcasm for me. Then she came to the part I had just read. "Well, that is very interesting! Nice work!"

"Yep, so it seems that the elder Avery did have a daughter who died."

"And now we need to find out who killed her, which is where Riles comes in."

"Bingo!" I said pointing my finger at her. Since we had a bit of time before we picked Riley up from school, I suggested some lunch. Nana said only if I paid, which I always did anyway, so I agreed.

During lunch at our usual haunt, Nana called and updated Dougie on what I had found, and I updated Steve as well. We were still on to go back to the Mayhew house to try and contact the little girl. She was the only one who could tell us who had killed her, why she had been killed, and hopefully lead us to some evidence to prove who killed her. Pretty sure the police couldn't arrest someone based on information from a ghost. We would need solid evidence to back it up.

Riley was waiting for us in front of the school, which was unusual. I glanced at the car clock; we were early so why was she waiting for us? I barely stopped the car before she jumped in and literally slammed the door. Okay, something was definitely up. I put the car in park. Nana and I both turned to her at the same time.

"Okay, what's up?" I asked gently, but sternly.

"Nothing. Can we just go?" This was so out of character for her, but I didn't want to push her. When she was ready to tell us, she would.

"Are you okay to go on the investigation?" I knew I was probably about to get blasted, but all she did was nod a yes.

Chapter Thirteen

When we arrived at the Mayhew house, Steve and his crew were already there. I thought it would be just the four of us. But I'm sure he had a good reason for bringing the guys. "Hey Colton," I said walking to the back of the van.

"Hey guys!" His cheerfulness was infectious, and I found myself smiling just from the greeting. One could tell Colton loved investigating.

"Who's the new person?" I asked, nodding to the guy who looked completely lost while fighting with computer cables and losing.

"Oh? That's Dustin," he said pulling out two big black cases marked camera equipment. "He's from another paranormal group that's based out of Oklahoma," Colton pulled out two more cases and sat them on the ground. "He's helping us on a couple of investigations this weekend." I remembered Steve saying something about Celeste, Tanner, and Tony working on another investigation this weekend so they had to call in someone from another organization to help with our investigation, which was last minute. Colton looked over at Dustin who was rolling out a long orange extension cord from what looked to me like something that would hold a water hose. "Steve thought it would be good for him to help with this investigation so he can get use to our way of doing things."

"Sounds like a good plan. Speaking of Steve, where is he?" He nodded toward the house. Me and Riley followed his nod and Dustin, who was headed inside with the extension cord was nipping at our heels. Nana made it clear she was only there for moral support and refused to go inside the house so she sat outside with Colton.

We found Steve and the owner Mr. Wilson talking in the living room. My guess was Steve was filling the elder man in on what was going on since we were last here, less the Brynn in jail incident. But he had to know about Walter's demise because Dougie had to get permission from him to enter the house and possibly dig.

"Hey Steve, Mr. Wilson." Riley waved and smiled.

"Hello ladies," Steve said, then turned to Mr. Wilson. "You remember Stephi and her daughter Riley, don't you?"

"Of course, I do!" the elderly man said offended, "I wouldn't forget to perdy ladies like these two." Um, did he just wink at us? Really? Riley and I gave him very weak smiles and I knew exactly what Riley was thinking…ewwwww!!!

"Yes, who could forget," Steve said looking at me and smiling. Okay, what had gotten over him all of a sudden? Why was he acting so weird around me?

I quickly changed the subject, "Yes, well thank you both very much. Um, Steve we really need to get started." I eyeballed him as if to say 'Stop!' He knew that look because he immediately fell into line.

"Well Mr. Wilson, we really appreciate you allowing us to come in again and on such short notice. This should be the last time we need to bother you. I'll let you know what we find, sound good."

"Sounds good to me," he said while looking at his keychain for the car key and walking toward the door, shakily I might add, like he was the last time we saw him. I got shivers thinking of him on the road, driving.

Steve was shaking his head and chuckling when he turned back to us. I was still wondering what was going through that brain of his looking at me like some lovestruck teenager when suddenly he did a hundred-degree turnaround on us and became professional.

"Okay girls, ready to get some answers?"

We were more than ready, we wanted answers and today we were going to get them. No one was leaving this house until we had all the answers. Riley and I followed Steve back outside to the van where Colton handed us each a video camera, an audio recorder, and a small flashlight. Steve was given the same equipment. It was decided that Colton and Dustin would monitor the computer screens in the van and Nana would of course stay with them. The boys in the van could watch us through the cameras that were set up throughout the house and could also let us know if any anomalies showed up. Steve, Riley, and myself would go inside and try to make contact with Elizabeth and Walter.

I looked over at Riley, "Ready?" I could tell she was nervous, but determined, even though she had not experienced any possessions since the first time we had visited the house she was still uneasy. There wouldn't be any spirit box sessions this time around, so we would be relying mainly on her and the audio recorders for any information or proof. Since arriving the sun had set and the guys had shut off the lights to the house. I always wondered why they investigated at night so once I asked Steve. He told me there were a lot of different reasons for investigating at night. One he wanted to keep the conditions the same as the entity manifested and two there was less going on at night than during the day. Less human interference and more spirit activity.

"Riley, why don't you ask Lizzie some questions? See if we can get some responses." Steve whispered to her.

Riley responded back with an 'okay'. We couldn't see each other because of the darkness so nodding was out of the question. I heard her click on the audio recorder Colton gave her but before she could ask a question she blurted out, "Oh and btw, she doesn't like to be called Lizzie. Her name is Elizabeth." It would seem Riley's spidey senses were in full bloom.

"Okay, my apologies Elizabeth," Steve said sincerely even though he had just been put in his place by a ghost via Riley.

"Let's get started," I took out my audio recorder, turned it on and pushed the record button. "This is Riley, Stephi, and Steve in the living room." Steve had his investigators start a recording with the area they were in for reference when the crew went through the data later on. "Elizabeth, we are here to help. But we need you to tell us what happened to you." I paused to allow a response, if there was a response. I continued, "Riley is here, do you remember Riley?" Another pause. "Can you tell us how you died?" I felt a hand grab my arm, it was cold, and I thought it was Riley trying to get my attention. I clicked the recorder off. "What is it Riley?"

"What is what?" I heard her ask.

"What did you need? You grabbed my arm."

"I'm not near you, Mom." She said. Now that I thought about it, she did sound like she was on the other side of the room.

"Then who just grabbed my arm? Was it you, Steve?" For some reason, I couldn't or wouldn't believe it was the ghost of Elizabeth that had grabbed me, even though I knew the little girl had possessed Riley. Why would she grab my arm?

113

"Not me. I'm on the other side of the sectional."

"So, the only other 'being' would be…Elizabeth?" I meant it as a statement, but it came out as a question.

"Play back the recording Mom," Riley said with a little too much enthusiasm for me.

I turned on my mini flashlight so I could see the buttons and rewinded the audio recorder, I stopped it just after I recorded our location. The machine buzzed to life and out came my voice asking the questions from earlier. *'Elizabeth, we are here to help. But we need you to tell us what happened to you."* Nothing. *'Riley is here, do your remember Riley?"* A faint voice said something that sounded like 'Riley' I looked up at Riley, she smiled back. My next question boomed from the machine. 'Can you tell us how you died?" It didn't take long before only one word came through and it there was no doubting what it was….'Matty.' I quickly clicked off the recorder and looked at Riley and then Steve.

"Did y'all hear what I did?" Riley nodded letting me know she had indeed heard what I had.

"Who's Matty?" Steve asked which confirmed he had also heard the same as us.

This changed everything! Had it been Matty who had killed Elizabeth? And why? Why would he hurt such a sweet little girl? I knew he was a womanizer, but a murderer. As if she had read my thoughts, Riley said, "Yes it was Matty."

"Did she tell you that?" I asked looking over at Riley.

"Yep."

"Uh, guys." Steve chimed in still wanting an answer to his question, "*Who* is Matty?"

I plopped down on the sectional. "Only the son of the most influential man in Springfield," I looked up at him. "Matthew Avery!"

"No shit!" His reaction wasn't unexpected, I was shocked as well. "What does he have to do with his sister and her death?"

"Dunno," I looked at Riley, "You got anything, baby girl?"

She shook her head. "Nope."

"And why did she touch me? Did she want something from me?" As if on cue a loud bang came somewhere above us. Was that Elizabeth?

The voice of Dustin boomed over the headsets we were wearing which made us all jump. "Steve, there's movement in the attic." After the last investigation, Steve thought it best to put a camera in the attic in case anything happened. Well, it did!

What was it with that damn attic? Couldn't anything happen down here? Steve radioed back that he was on it as we all started toward the attic stairs. Friggin' house with its friggin' attic! While I was grumbling about the attic, Riley was power walking to the attic. Really? We reached the attic and Steve pulled down the door with the ladder as quietly and carefully as he could. As he started up the stairs, I grabbed his arm and at that moment, I don't know why, but I was genuinely scared for him. It was the same feeling I would get whenever Bill would leave for his shift. I whispered, "*Be careful!*" He laid his hand on mine, and I knew he understood. For some reason, I didn't want to let go, again I don't know why, so I held onto his hand. Riley grabbed the back of my shirt, letting me know

115

she was there. As we made our way up the stairs another bang even louder than the first rang out and we froze. Wait, there was a rhythm to the bangs, like someone hitting a wall. Dustin's voice boomed over the headsets once again and once again we jumped. "Steve, move cautiously. There is someone up there and it's not a ghost."

I looked down at Riley. "Stay behind me and stay close," I whispered, and she nodded. I moved the small flashlight back toward Steve and we started moving again. The rhythmic bangs continued without missing a beat. Who could it be? Brynn was still being held down at the police station. We knew Walter was toast, so it couldn't be him. Well, it could be, but only in ghost form. As we crested the top of the stairs I saw a black figure wielding something against the wall. The ominous figure didn't seem to notice us. Maybe Colton was wrong about it being human and was actually a residual spirit that is tied to a specific location. Like Walter perhaps? This was his home, but why would he be hitting the wall? And could a ghost even do that? Steve flipped the light switch before I could ask him. I didn't have to see the shock on our faces, I could feel it. Colton had been right, it was human and the human was someone I never expected to see. Standing across from us, holding a sledgehammer and knocking a huge hole in the wall was…Matty Avery. We all stood there, frozen until…he turned toward us with a crazed, madman look that frankly scared the bejesus out of me. In fear for our lives I shoved Riley behind me and reached in the back of my jeans and pulled out my Colt, this time the safety was not on. I pointed it toward the floor but was ready to shoot if needs be. First I wanted to try and reason with him.

"Matty?" I moved a little closer.

Riley grabbed my arm, "Mom."

116

I nodded it was okay. "Matty, it's me, Stephi. Remember me?" He lowered the sledgehammer, not as much as I would want, but even just that little bit let me know he understood me. "We went to school together Matty." He lowered the sledgehammer a bit more.

"Stephi? Stephi Lane?" By using my maiden name, I knew he was thinking back to those days in school.

"Yeah, Matty. It's me." Seeing I could reason with him somewhat, I felt it safe enough to tell Riley to text Nana to call Dougie. "Whatcha doing up here?" I asked trying to keep it calm and relaxed.

He turned toward the wall and looked at the hole he had made, then looked at the sledgehammer in his hand. The look on his face turned to pure shock and he dropped the hammer. He looked over at us, "What happened? What am I doing here?"

I flipped the safety on the Colt and put it back in my jeans, "We were hoping you could tell us." It was like a switch had flipped on and he was once again the Matty I knew from school. He moved over to an old rocking chair and sat putting his head in his hands. He looked like he was trying to shake off a bad night of drinking. "What is the last thing you remember?" I asked moving toward him.

"I remember getting into town, not that I wanted to be back in this rathole of a town." Okay, I was going to ignore that. "But my father wanted me back, so I did as I was ordered. I remember getting off the plane. After that, I don't remember anything until you snapped me out of whatever trance I was in."

"Did he say why he wanted you to come home?"

"This town is NOT my home!"

I raised my hands, "Okay, sorry."

"He didn't say why he wanted me back, he just ordered me to come back." The loathing for his father was evident not only in his voice, but also on his face. A realization came to him, "What are all of you doing here?"

Well, that was a question that could be answered, but would he believe us? Probably not. He would most likely laugh at us. "Well," I looked over at Riley and Steve, "we're here to investigate." Keeping it vague at the moment was a cop-out, but I wasn't in the mood to be laughed at right now. When he persisted, I knew he was back to his old self.

"Investigate what?"

"A murder, of sorts." While I was trying to be vague, Riley wasn't having any of it.

"We are here to investigate the murder of Elizabeth," she said point blank, no fluff, just come right out and say it. Unfortunately, she didn't stop there, "And the murder of Walter Mayhew."

Steve and I both looked over at Matty who had turned so white that he looked like a ghost. Well, that said a lot! So, I went a step further, "Matty, do you know anything about the death of Elizabeth and Walter?"

"I-I don't want to say anything without a lawyer." He was scared, that was apparent.

"Okay, understood. But can you explain what you meant by being in a trance?" When he had said it earlier it didn't register, but thinking back on when we first found him it did seem like he was in a trance.

"It felt like I wasn't myself, like someone else was forcing me to knock out a hole in that wall. And I don't even remember how I got here." He looked around, "Where am I anyway?"

It was Steve's turn to chime in, "The house that Walter Mayhew was renting, along with his fiancé Brynn."

As always, Dougie had impeccable timing. "Why are y'all still up here?"

I didn't want to say in front of Matty that we had stayed up here because we were recording everything that happened. I would tell Dougie later. "Uh, we were just chatting." Seriously, chatting? I couldn't think of anything else better to say than chatting! Dougie knew me too well to believe that baloney.

"Right." He said looking directly at me with a raised eyebrow. He then turned to Matty flipping open his ID, "Mr. Avery, I need you to come to the station with me." At first he looked like he wanted to resist but chose not to probably because he was too exhausted from everything else that had happened. Matty shook his head actually looking relieved to be leaving the house, but not what lie ahead.

"Matty, it's going to be okay. We'll figure this out, okay?" I put my arm on his shoulder. I was expecting him to pull away, but he didn't. Again, he just shook his head. I watched as they slowly made their way down the attic stairs then turned back to Steve and Riley. "What is it about this attic?" I walked over to the hole Matty had decoratively banged out. Clearly, he was looking for something.

"It's not the attic, mom," Riley said coming up next to me. "It's Elizabeth."

"Elizabeth?" I got closer to the hole, there was something inside. "How could it be the little girl?" I pulled out my small flashlight and shined it into the darkness. What the hell? I moved the light closer and froze. "Oh, shit!" I couldn't believe what I was looking at. "I think we need the police to come back."

"Why? What did you find?" Steve asked moving closer to us.

"Elizabeth," Riley said before I could reply.

"Wanna hear my theory?" I asked looking from the hole to them. They both shook their heads. "Riley did Elizabeth, and correct me if I'm wrong, possess him like she did you and brought him here to knock a hole in the wall so that we would find her remains. I know it sounds out there, but then when is dealing with ghosts it's not that far out there?"

Riley smiled. "You got it, mom," she said while texting Nana once again who answered back that she had gone down to the station with Dougie and would have the station send a crime unit to the house.

"So, we found the little girl's remains, but what about Walter Mayhew and the painting?" Steve pointed out. "Isn't that also the reason we were investigating the house."

"Yeah, good point." I said, "but can we please get out of this cursed attic especially since it's a crime scene now."

After we climbed down the stairs we gathered by the van which was also the command center. We still needed to find the painting, which was the real case here, and find Walter Mayhew. I remembered Riley had seen Walter's ghost with the painting, however she didn't say where she saw him. "Riley, when you saw Walter and the painting where was he?"

"Like was he outside or inside?"

"Well, yes to both of those. But where was he? Was he here or at the museum…"

"Mom," she said in a sarcastic tone, "of course, I saw him here, the video was from the house."

"Well, yeah okay," I admitted reluctantly. I couldn't help when I had brain farts. They just happened! "So where did you see him?"

"It was…" she looked at Steve, then at me. "…in the attic."

Oh lord! Of course, it would be the attic. Why wouldn't it be? I was really beginning to dislike that part of the house. We trudged back up to the attic even though we shouldn't since it was a crime scene, so we agreed we would just stay on the opposite side. "Okay, everyone take a wall. Holler if you find something." I said picking the wall that was on the same wall as Elizabeth's remains. Riley took the back wall and Steve the wall opposite me. Well, at least we could do this investigation with the lights on. I started by knocking on the wall, if the area behind the wall was hollow the sound would be less dense and make an echoing sound. I heard the other two follow suit and the sound of all of us knocking could be heard all the way down to the van, according to Colton. Pfft, of course, he could, we still had our headphones on. We were all rhythmically knocking when suddenly someone hit a different beat. I knew it wasn't me, so I turned to look. It was Riley who left her post at her wall and headed for the sledgehammer Matty had been using earlier.

"No, Riley!" I shouted, a little too high that it came out as a screech. "That's evidence." Steve and I started looking around for something we could pry the boards from the wall frame.

"Here," Steve said producing a crowbar. "Show me where you heard the hollow part Riley." She pointed to a part of the wall that looked off, but unless you got close to it, you wouldn't notice it. Steve wedged the crowbar under one of the planks and yanked. The board moved surprisingly easy, so much so it took him off guard and he almost knocked us over. Instinctively Riley and I moved to catch him if he fell. He brushed himself off and went for the other planks. This time it wasn't the planks attempting to knock him over it was a dead body. Walter Mayhew's dead body to be exact. I grabbed Riley and she grabbed me. Steve on the other hand looked up at us, "A little help, please!" We both took one of his arms and let the body plop to the floor. "Well, we found Walter." And then...

"What are you three doing up here?" Dougie and the Crime Scene Unit poured into the attic like a tsunami. Nana was bringing up the rear. Ghosts she wouldn't have anything to do with, but dead bodies and bones she was in hog heaven.

"Uh, well..." I started and he interrupted me. I could feel my mom's eyes boring into me. I knew she would be yelling at me later about disturbing a crime scene. Not looking forward to that little chat.

"And who is that?!" he asked pointing to the dead body crumpled on the floor.

"Walter Mayhew," Riley said matter of factly.

"We had this theory," I began lamely I might add, "well, remembering what Riley caught from the investigation," I looked over at her," we thought maybe Walter's body might be up here too." I tried to be as vague as possible but telling him in front of the whole CSI unit would make us sound insane. "And, well, we were right."

122

"Stephi, I want all three of you out of here, now!" Dougie was pretty easy-going the majority of the time except when it came to his job. He did things by the book, as did Nana, and he didn't like anyone, even me, messing around his crime scenes. We could have contaminated a key piece of evidence.

Riley and Steve bolted, wimps! As I walked past Dougie I gave him my best 'I'm sorry' look. Nana on the other hand had the look of the devil. Before I went down the attic steps, I turned to them, "You might want to check the wall Walter fell out of…the painting might be in there."

I found the gang back at the van. They were all a buzz about the other dead body and how we got busted. "Hopefully the painting is in that wall."

"Well, it was." My mom's voice made me cringe. I turned to face the music and get my butt whoopin' over with.

"That's great news!" I said smiling my biggest fake smile.

"Yes, I suppose it is," she said saddling up next to me and whispered in my ear. "If you ever pull a stunt like that again, I'll pull you from the business. Are we clear?"

"Nana! Mom wasn't the only one that went up there." When Riley was fired up, you wanted her to be on your side. And thank goodness she was.

"Riley Ann Cay," You knew when Nana used your full name you were about to go to war. "I don't expect you to know the consequences of disturbing a crime scene, but your mother does. It's the number one rule of investigating. No one goes near it until the police have finished!"

"I think I have lived with enough police officers in my life to know the 'consequences' of 'disturbing a crime scene'" she was using her fingers as quotation marks to emphasize her words. "And besides we were on the 'other' side of the attic, away from the bones."

"None of you had any business up there Riley!"

"Uh, yes we did Nana! We were working on the case we were hired to do. Find Walter Mayhew, find the painting! And we did!"

"Ma, we had already contaminated that scene the last time we were in the attic, when we found Matty." Sometimes rationalizing with her calmed her down. I was hoping this was one of those times. "Look I know it was wrong to go up there, but we had a hunch Walter would be up there."

"Nana," Riley had calmed down as well. "Why are you so mad about us being up there? I also know it was wrong but to threaten Mom like that."

"Because it's possible Matty might be responsible for both Elizabeth's and Walter's deaths."

Okay, didn't see that coming, but that's why we worked so well together. "Huh, why do you think he killed both of them?"

"Not think, Stephi, we know he did."

"How?"

"Once Brynn found out Matty had been brought in she spilled her guts." She walked over to the van and sat down. She looked a little pale. Before I could say anything she continued. "Apparently Matty and Brynn have been working together for some time now. The Brynn and Walter wedding was a front. She's got engaged to

Matty so he would help her steal the painting." She paused and took a few deep breaths.

"Ma, are you okay?" I said before she could say anything.

She waved her hand at me as if to say I'm fine and continued, "They planned the murder of Elizabeth because Matty didn't want an illegitimate child to get, what he called, his inheritance." She asked Colton for some water, took a sip and continued, "So, they drowned her and boarded up her body in the wall so no one would find her."

"But wouldn't someone smell the decaying body?" I asked what everyone was thinking. "And why in this house? How long had Brynn and Walter lived here?"

"The house was originally owned by Mr. Avery, but he sold it to the old geezer who shouldn't drive which stood empty until the purchase."

"His name is Mr. Wilson," I corrected.

"Whatever," she rolled her eyes at me and continued. "Mainly Avery had it as a write-off for taxes. So, by the time he sold the house, the smell would have dissipated." She took another sip of water. "Brynn and Walter haven't lived here for very long. But Elizabeth was killed when the elder Avery owned the house which was about roughly ten years ago."

"So why was the painting stolen?" Riley asked.

"Matty didn't want a shrine hanging in the museum, or again what he called his inheritance. Which upon the elder Avery's death he would get everything, museum included."

"So, Walter was expendable," I said more to myself than anyone standing around me. "Poor guy. I wonder if he knew his whole engagement was a farce or even worse that his fake fiancé and her real fiancé were going to murder him."

"We'll never know," Nana said.

"We could do another spirit box session," Riley suggested.

"Yeah, right! No way. I don't want to know that bad." I said laughing. "Well, we can't do anything else here." I glanced over at Ma who looked like she was about to pass out. "Let's get out of here." Everyone agreed. Steve said not to worry about helping with the equipment. Apparently, he saw how out of sorts Nana was. I thanked him and told him to let me know if anything else happens before they leave.

When we arrived home, I had Riley take Nana to her room while I put the teapot on to make some tea. Her suddenly becoming ill had me concerned, very concerned. This is a woman who never got sick, until she was diagnosed with cancer. It was one of the darkest days of my life. She would reassure me by saying 'Don't worry, I've got this beat.' And she did for the longest time. But the chemotherapy and radiation took its toll on her. She was sick, weak and for the longest time, I thought the chemo and radiation would kill her and not the cancer. The teapot whistled startling me out of my thoughts. I put a tea bag in a coffee cup and poured the hot water over it, my thoughts taking over again while I waited for the tea to steep. What if she was seriously ill? I don't think I could take losing her. It took everything out of me losing Bill and all these years later, I still have nightmares. Once again I was jolted from my thoughts, only this time it was Riley and not the tea kettle.

"Penny for your thoughts," she said with a smirk.

126

I glanced back at her and smiled. "Want some tea?" She nodded and sat down at the table.

"How is she doing?" I asked, afraid of the answer.

"Better. Her color has come back. She dozed off as soon as her head hit the pillow."

"That's good. It's been a stressful day." Riley could tell I was just talking, that my thoughts were far away from our conversation.

"It's back," Riley said.

"What's back?" I knew the answer even before she made the comment.

"The cancer."

"How do you know?" Again, I knew the answer before she said it.

"Elizabeth told me," she said blankly. "When we were at the house today, Elizabeth spoke to me. I had a feeling that day you picked me up from school." Ah, so that is why she was so distant. "And Nana has known it for a while now."

Tears welled up in my eyes but didn't overflow. Yet. "She won't go through that hell again Riley. You know that, right?"

"I know," she said in a shaky voice, and I could see tears starting to form in her eyes.

"So, you know this time we will lose her."

Riley couldn't speak, she could only vigorously shake her head in agreement. The tears were flowing from both of us like someone turned on a faucet. I was immediately by her side, comforting her as she did me when her dad passed away. She was my rock that day and many days thereafter. Now it was my turn to be her rock. She loved her Nana and losing her would be one of the worst days of her life next to losing her dad. We held each other for I don't know how long and frankly didn't care. We would be losing the one person that was our rock, the backbone of our family even before I married Bill. When we finally broke apart, we were a mess. Eyes all red, snot running from our noses, and we laughed at the sight of one another. We knew in that moment we would fight…fight for Nana.

www.ingramcontent.com/pod-product-compliance
Lightning Source LLC
Chambersburg PA
CBHW052006220626
47052CB00004B/1115